"You're Going To Freeze Out Here, Caitlin."

Michael drew Cait's coat around her and brushed a soft kiss across her forehead. Too much, too soon, he thought. He was pushing her too hard and he knew it, but he'd never met a woman like this. He'd never *wanted* a woman like this. His instincts were convinced this was the right time, but he knew he couldn't ask her to do anything she didn't want to do. Despite his hesitation, he pulled her against him.

Cait burrowed into his warmth. For another moment, they simply breathed together. The scent of him drove her crazy....

"Caitlin," he whispered. "Invite me inside for coffee."

"I can't." She sighed deeply and closed her eyes, well aware he wasn't really asking for coffee. He rubbed her shoulders, let his hands smooth her back, and it felt so good. "I only have instant," she replied, weakening.

"I'm not picky."

Dear Reader:

Welcome to Silhouette Desire—sensual, compelling, believable love stories written by and for today's woman. When you open the pages of a Silhouette Desire, you open yourself up to a new world—a world of promising passion and endless love.

Each and every Silhouette Desire is a wonderful love story that is both sensual *and* emotional. You're with the hero and heroine each and every step of the way—from their first meeting, to their first kiss . . . to their happy ending. You'll experience all the deep joys—and occasional tribulations—of falling in love.

In future months, look for terrific Silhouette Desire romances from some of your favorite authors, such as Annette Broadrick, Dixie Browning, Nancy Martin and Lass Small, just to name a few.

So go wild with Desire. You'll be glad you did!

Lucia Macro
Senior Editor

SUSAN MEIER

TAKE THE RISK

SILHOUETTE *Desire*

Published by Silhouette Books New York

America's Publisher of Contemporary Romance

SILHOUETTE BOOKS
300 East 42nd St., New York, N.Y. 10017

ISBN: 0-373-05567-6

First Silhouette Books printing May 1990

SUSAN MEIER

is a wife, mother, legal secretary and romance writer. She firmly believes that, in romance, sometimes it's not what you say but how you say it. Therefore, the most simple events can be made to sound beautiful.

When she's not writing or working she's probably watching movies, which she counts as one of her greatest interests, or reading. In addition to category romance, Susan likes books that combine science fiction with love.

One

Red alert! Red alert!''

Michael Flannery wished somebody had yelled that at about ten o'clock this morning, right after his cousin Kiki entered his office chattering about her latest "idea." Then, he wouldn't be sitting in Catz's bar, feeling like a troll for bursting her bubble again.

Chairs screeched across the floor as the card game behind Michael disbursed in short order. He swiveled his stool around and watched as the afternoon's winner shoved money into his jeans pockets, while the loser slid the cards under the poker machine. A girlie magazine flew over Michael's head, was deftly caught by the burly bartender and was crammed between two rows of tall, dark beer bottles in a glass-doored cooler. In the midst of the ruckus, a huge man with solemn eyes quietly walked from the back of the room, took the tape out of the VCR and hid it behind a mirror.

Michael sighed and reached for his beer. It was pretty obvious the bar was about to be raided by somebody's wife or mother and these gentlemen were simply taking care of business. But even with the present clamor, this was a normal bar full of normal guys who were doing normal things. Unfortunately, Kiki thought she'd discovered something unique. He'd hated explaining to her that there was nothing newsworthy about this place, nothing worth featuring in a magazine. But the hard part was explaining that she was the oddball. He tried to be delicate, but there was just no way around the fact that she needed to readjust her thinking. She was a rich kid who led a sheltered life, and she had an unusual perception of normal. And if she wanted to be the person who chose the stories for the magazine *Flannery's Place*, she'd have to start thinking like an average resident of Riverside, not like one of the rich ones.

Difficult as it was explaining all this, it was nothing compared to what Michael felt when she burst into tears. But the real killer was that he couldn't go after her when, a few minutes ago, she ran out of the bar sobbing. She wanted a real job in the real world and he'd given her one. Now they'd both suffer the consequences until she either succeeded or quit trying.

A hush fell over the crowd as ten meaty men quieted in their seats. Michael glanced out the window and saw a slip of a woman heading toward the bar. He could only make out impressions in the twilight, but the fiery hue of her hair was unmistakable. Normally, he would have guessed that the "red" in red alert identified the intruder for the regulars and clued them in on who had to be on their best behavior. But then a quick glance around showed everybody looked nervous and every activity had been stored, hidden or at the very least stopped. This woman appeared to be trouble for everybody.

Stash, the bartender, confidently swiped down the smudgy bar with a ratty-looking cloth, but when he looked up from his task and saw the television, he swore.

"Quick, somebody change that channel!"

Too late, Michael thought, grinning because he was beginning to see the humor in the situation. It had been a long time—perhaps the whole way back to college—since he'd let his hair down and enjoyed the camaraderie and silliness of a neighborhood bar. It wasn't a practice he'd want to resume on a regular basis, but one night of craziness didn't hurt anybody. In fact, after his episode with Kiki, he needed some harmless fun.

The door of the bar burst open and an absolutely beautiful woman entered. Michael's first thought was that distance didn't do her justice. Her hair was as bright as autumn leaves and her green eyes packed enough sparkle to knock a man right off his bar stool. She blew in with a gust of blustery November air, but Michael didn't feel the icy wind. He was so surprised and impressed by her looks that he didn't even notice that she held a heaping plate covered by a red-and-white checkered napkin or that the once boisterous bar was now eerily quiet.

With one sweep of his eyes, he took in her glorious shoulder-length hair, her simple gray wool jacket and her form-hugging jeans. The fit of her clothes accented every enticing curve she had, the same way an hourglass molded sand, but her full, pouty mouth, pert nose and crystal-clear eyes were just as appealing as her perfect body.

No one spoke, no one moved, and life seemed to be caught in freeze-frame. Then a rousing cheer erupted from the television and even Michael tensed as the woman's attention flew to the screen, especially when she narrowed her eyes into green slits after one glance at the TV.

"So, Stash," she said. Her words rang ominously in the awesome stillness, but there was an unmistakable twitching of her mouth, as if she was desperately fighting a smile. "I see you're up to your old tricks again."

As she glided past Michael, the scent of spicy chicken wafted through the stench of cigarettes, beer and sweat. In the next second, sweet musky perfume floated around him. It wasn't cloying, it wasn't flowery, it was just appealing. He inhaled again, then twisted his chair imperceptibly so he could continue watching her.

She politely passed the plate to the bartender but clicked her tongue with disapproval. "Half-naked women mud wrestling," she scorned, then turned and began unbuttoning her coat. "Really, Stash!"

She tossed her coat over the antlers of one of six deer heads mounted as trophies on the back wall, sauntered to the bar, slid under the gate and ambled to the TV. With one crisp smack she silenced the machine, then ducked under the gate again and began walking to the poker machine.

"Come on, Cait!" Stash moaned, reddening with discomfort. "This is a bar, for Pete's sake!"

Hands on her hips, Cait spun to face the bartender, but she was smiling fiendishly. "Oh, and I suppose having a liquor license gives you permission to do anything you want?" she asked sarcastically, then bent and grabbed the plug of the brightly lit electronic game. "You might think so, but I'm absolutely positive the Pennsylvania Liquor Control Board forbids gambling."

"That machine doesn't pay out," Stash lied with a sheepish grin, but Cait silenced him with an all-knowing look, even as she yanked the plug from the wall. Colorful lights instantly blackened and the man who'd racked up enough points for a secret payoff swore ripely under his breath.

"Sis, will you get home?" Stash yelped, leveling her with a look of total exasperation.

"Now, now, Stash, don't be so grouchy," Cait chastised, dusting her hands as if she'd just performed a totally distasteful task. "Just think of me as your guardian angel."

"Go home!"

"No," she said and strolled to the bar again.

Michael put his elbow on the bar and rested his chin on his closed fist, enjoying himself immensely. Now, this was a real woman. If anybody ever spoke to Kiki in that tone of voice—even one of her brothers—she'd faint, and when she came to she'd die. For a whole new set of reasons, he wished Kiki hadn't burst into tears and run off.

"Mom wants me to bring her dish home," Caitlin said as she took the seat offered to her by a young guy who looked as if he was about to hyperventilate. She smiled at the kid and he darted away with his beer. Michael noticed that Cait watched him until he eventually settled for standing room at the end of the bar. Michael gauged the kid's age to be twenty-one and a day, and the look on Cait's face said she also came to the conclusion that the guy was old enough to be drinking. She turned to her brother again. "In fact, I'm supposed to get the ones from last night and the night before, too."

"Okay," Stash reluctantly agreed. "Want a beer or something while you wait?"

She ran a hand through her hair and Michael watched her red curls as they picked up the light from a bar lamp. "No," she said and glanced around again. "If I do, I can get it myself."

As she said the last, her gaze meandered to Michael and she faltered before quickly pivoting away. Michael looked down at his tweed vest, then turned his attention to his rolled-up shirtsleeves. Even with his jacket removed and his tie open, he supposed he looked more than a little out of place. It was no wonder she looked away. He'd probably shocked her.

Obviously bored, she looked around again. "So, Stash, what other decadence did you have on the agenda for tonight?"

"You know, Caitlin," Stash said, drumming a half-eaten chicken leg on the edge of his plate in a show of dwindling patience. "If you don't like it here, you can always leave."

"I can't leave," she reminded him, sighing. "I have to take your plate home. Honestly, Stash, can't you guys think of something constructive to do in here so I won't be so bored while I wait for your dishes?''

"Like what?" Stash muttered in exasperation.

"There's always poker," Michael said because he couldn't resist the urge to tease her. She'd dished out enough when she marched into the place and with a crowd like this Michael assumed she had to be able to take it, too.

Cait took the bait and spun to face Michael. "Poker is not constructive."

"Sure it is," Michael disagreed with a smile. "It teaches logic, helps a man learn how to figure odds, read his opponent and hold his temper if he's smart."

Stash obviously caught on to what Michael was doing and he burst out laughing, but Cait gave Michael a puzzled frown.

"And there's nothing wrong with mud wrestling, either. It's better than porno movies on the VCR."

Finally comprehending, Cait's eyes widened comically. "Stash, you didn't!"

Stash sort of shrugged, then grinned sheepishly.

"I'm afraid he did," Michael advised her with mock gravity.

Cait hid her face in her hands. "Oh, Lord, let's hope Mom doesn't find out."

"My guess is she won't," Michael said with a chuckle. "Unless she looks under the poker machine for the cards or behind the mirror for the videotape."

Caitlin broke into giggles. "You guys are terrible!"

"Normal, human, typical," Michael interjected, totally pleased that she accepted him, maybe even liked him. He certainly liked her. Everything about her. Right from her shiny red hair to her scruffy tennis shoes. "But not terrible. By the way, I'm Michael Flannery."

Caitlin automatically took the hand he'd extended. Normally, she didn't talk to strangers, especially not men who happened into the bar, but she liked this guy. Never mind that she generally didn't trust good-looking men. This one had a sense of humor and that made up for a multiplicity of sins, as far as Caitlin was concerned.

"I'm Caitlin Petrunak and this is my brother, Stash. That guy in the back is my cousin, Bear."

Michael Flannery smiled at her, and Caitlin got goose bumps the whole way to her toes. It wasn't from the warm look in his soft brown eyes. It wasn't because he was just plain gorgeous with his wavy black hair and dimples. There was something about him, some odd kind of magnetism or charisma.

His suit jacket had been removed and hung over the back of his chair. Though his tweed vest was still buttoned, his tie hung loose. The sleeves of his white shirt were rolled to his elbows, revealing muscular forearms peppered with rich black hair which was as glossy as the thick hair on his head. He was a rare combination of masculinity and old-money sophistication that somehow meshed into a very sexy, intelligent and intriguing man.

Without warning his gaze met hers. His dark, compelling eyes were set in a face she found fascinating, not just handsome. Sturdy came to mind, then uncompromising, then dangerous. One corner of his smooth mouth was poised in amusement, but the twinkle in his eyes had nothing to do with humor. He was giving her that look . . . that unexplainable, undefinable look a man gives a woman when he's interested in her as a woman, not a person....

"If you'll excuse me," Caitlin said as she rose from her stool, "I think I'll clean some glasses for Stash."

"What for?" Stash asked. "You never do any other time."

"Well, I'm going to tonight."

It took a minute, but Stash saw through her ploy like a newly washed window. "Nah!" He batted a hand. "There aren't even three dirty glasses back here." He grinned devilishly. "Sit!"

Reluctantly, Caitlin sat. There wasn't anything else she could do, unless she wanted it obvious that she was running away from the charmer beside her. She took a deep breath and glanced down at the chipped wood of the bar.

"So," Michael asked, leaning forward, looking relaxed and comfortable and making her feel a tad trapped. "What do you do when you're not feeding your brother?"

Cautiously, she peeked at him. She wasn't the type to be rude to anybody, but there was a line and he'd crossed it just by the way he was looking at her. And unless he stopped, she couldn't even talk to him. "I'm an accountant."

"Certified public accountant," Stash qualified proudly. "And a modest one. Works for Barnhart Steel. Manages taxes or tax shelters—or are you in investments now?"

Michael's brows rose. "You work for Barnhart Steel?"

"Yes."

Her answer was just as clipped and snappy as the way she bounced off her seat. Michael stared after her, wondering what happened to the sweet woman who'd introduced herself to him only two minutes before. He seriously considered finishing his beer and leaving, and then he remembered Kiki and the story she swore floated in the air of this bar. Suddenly, he got the same sensation. Every nerve ending in his body sprang to life and his heart thumped. There was no greater stimulant to a reporter than a story, but a story about a pretty woman was even better. He scrambled off his seat and caught her arm.

"That's pretty impressive."

"My brother exaggerates my importance," Caitlin said, yanking on her arm, but Michael held her fast.

"Uh-uh," he disagreed, then slid his fingers up and down her arms, watching the way the simplest touch made her eyes widen and the way she sucked in her breath. He wondered if she was running from the same attraction he wanted to pursue, then decided that it made more sense for her to be running because she was hiding something. "Only the best work for Barnhart Steel. Everybody knows that."

"Cait didn't get a job she wanted," Stash called down the bar, obviously following the conversation and his sister, talking for her when she wouldn't speak for herself. "Now she's a little defensive."

"Will you shut up?" Caitlin moaned, but Stash pretended not to hear her.

"She's the best," he went on. Michael tightened his hold on Caitlin's arm, afraid that if he let her go she'd make a beeline for the door. "Graduated in the upper half of her class. Had three job offers here in Riverside before the end of her last semester. Took the one with the mill because it paid the most. In fact, she earns a king's ransom."

Jerking out of Michael's hold, Caitlin said, "I'm going to count to three, and then I'm going to call Bear." She pointed to the huge man in the back, the one with coal-black hair everywhere, even on his knuckles. Her green eyes grew enormous and glittered with anger.

Michael immediately dropped her arm, not because of her threat to call Bear but because he couldn't believe he'd held on to her against her wishes. He thought perhaps he was losing his marbles, then realized not one person in the room even glanced in their direction. She had a brother and a cousin in this room. Shouldn't somebody have done something to come to her rescue? No, maybe not. They were probably getting even with her for tormenting them when she walked in. In fact, it looked as though setting her up with him was the nastiest trick they could think of to pull against her. Michael considered that he should be insulted; then he realized he'd played right into their hands.

"What makes you so sure your cousin would have jumped to your aid?"

His question stopped her dead in her tracks and the look she gave him was one of total confusion.

"Because Bear's tonight's bouncer—"

"After the way you teased these guys when you came in, I think they figured they owed you one."

"Owed me one?" she interrupted, laughing.

"Yeah. For turning off the television and pulling the plug on their gambling."

"They might have thought it was funny to watch you pester me," she conceded. "But they weren't paying me back for anything. One word from me and Bear would have shown you the street from a new angle."

"Oh, I don't know," Michael countered, still noting that Bear was far, far away, Stash was eating and the rest of the boys were watching television. "From the looks of things, they're still a little angry with you for spoiling their fun."

"They can't be mad at me," she said, sounding oddly surprised and amused by his conclusion. "I own this bar. I—"

Caitlin clasped her hand over her mouth just as ten beer glasses hit the bar with a thud and everybody in the room looked at Stash. Stash cursed roundly under his breath, slapping his hands on the bar and looking as though he was about to leap over it.

Instantly Michael tensed for a fight, knowing he was about to be beaten to a pulp even though he hadn't the slightest idea why. Everything he did in this bar seemed to get him into trouble. And the worst of it was, he was too old for this stuff.

As he held his breath and waited, hoping he really wouldn't have to defend himself in this bar full of guys who looked as if they ate raw meat for lunch, the biggest one, the one with hair on his knuckles and biceps like tree trunks, moved from the back of the room and stood right beside Cait.

Michael backed off, holding up both hands. "Uh . . . sorry, guys . . . uh, just, uh, trying to get to know the lady."

"This lady doesn't want to get to know you," Cait informed him softly, laying a hand on the enormous forearm of the guy who was two heads taller than she.

Bear studied Cait for a minute, then glanced over her head. "Stash?"

Tapping his fingers on the bar, Stash considered Michael before he looked at Bear. "Go finish your beer," he ordered gruffly.

Michael's breath rushed out in a noisy gust. Everybody in the bar went back to drinking. Tugging the front of his vest into place, Michael decided to finish his beer just to prove he wasn't a chicken, then beat a hasty retreat because he wasn't a fool. He was getting out of here while he still had his sanity and all his teeth.

As he reached for his glass, the man sitting on the stool beside him asked the bartender, "How 'bout a draft, Stash?"

Cautiously, Michael lifted his eyes to follow Stash's movements and when he did he saw Caitlin put her hand on Stash's arm. "You finish eating," she instructed him softly. "I'll get Tom's beer."

Michael wouldn't have thought that strange, except Stash jerked his arm away from Cait's hand and sucked in a breath as he glared at her. Totally and thoroughly confused, Michael cocked his head and watched Stash amble over to his chicken while Cait slid under the gate and poured Tom's draft. Clearing her throat, she placed the drink in front of Tom and when she did, Michael caught her arm.

"What the hell was that all about?" he whispered. Stash had to be six foot three, which made Bear six foot six, which made Michael more than a little nervous. Particularly since he had a good ten years on both of them.

"None of your business," Caitlin replied, walking away.

When she returned with her customer's change, Michael grabbed her arm again. "He wasn't protecting your honor," Michael challenged. "He was mad at you. But I was the one who would have been beaten. I think I at least have the right to know why."

"Trust me, you really don't want to know."

But he did. Trouble or not, he desperately wanted to know why every man in this room wanted to take a swipe at him, and he wouldn't rest until knew this bar's secret. There wasn't just a story here; there was a hot potato. Something so good these people wanted to keep it hidden. Which was exactly why he wanted to print it. "Is there a reason I shouldn't?" he inquired offhandedly, but he studied her closely.

"A very good one," Caitlin replied, smiling sweetly just before she turned to go.

Michael spun her around again. "And that reason is?"

Cait sighed tiredly. "Don't you get the message, buddy?"

"No. So why don't you tell me?" He nodded at Stash. "Whisper. He'll never hear. He's not paying any attention."

"No!" She glanced around and saw the room had returned to normal. Everybody was either watching TV or talking. It was obvious that no one would notice she was speaking with him. She sighed again and faced him. "Look, there are some things we don't talk about in here." She took a step closer and lowered her voice. "One of which is that the bar is owned by a w-o-m-a-n."

Michael would have laughed, but she was deadly serious. He frowned and whispered, "So?"

"So, the twentieth century has not found its way to this side of the river yet. In case you hadn't noticed," she added, nodding at the mounted deer and bear heads on the far wall.

"But even *Gunsmoke* had Miss Kitty," Michael protested. He was getting that sick feeling in the pit of his stomach, the one he always got when a story didn't pan out.

"Yes, but Miss Kitty wasn't the only one in town who had a job. Matt Dillon was the sheriff, Festus was a deputy and Doc, well, I think you get the picture."

He smiled sort of sheepishly, sort of hopefully. "Not really."

She sighed with disgust. "In here," she said, her voice oozing with strained patience, "Bear and Stash are the only ones who have full-time jobs because they're actually employees of the bar. It's their job to be here and they wouldn't be here if I wouldn't have bought the bar. The rest of these guys work for the mill, but only when they're called."

"What do you mean, when they're called?"

"What planet are you from, buddy? Don't you know anything?"

"Humor me," Michael said, smiling again. She was so astounded he didn't understand the local life-style that she seemed to have forgotten she didn't want to tell him this stuff.

"They work six weeks or six months or even six years, but they can get laid off for six weeks or six months or six years...."

"Six years?"

"Sometimes more."

"That's not much of a job," he commented.

"That's my point."

"So?"

"So what?" she said, clearly exasperated.

"What does that have to do with you?" Michael asked, keeping his voice low, cooperating with her unspoken rules of quiet and privacy so that they wouldn't disturb the normal atmosphere of the bar again—and he wouldn't risk getting everybody mad again.

"Not only am I a full-time employee of Barnhart Steel," she said, her voice low, "but I'm at the top. In management."

"So they hate you?"

She glared at him. "No, they do not hate me. They just resent me."

"For what?" he asked.

"What is this, *20 Questions*?"

"I told you, I'm just curious. After all, your problem almost got me punched. I want to be sure to avoid it in the future."

"Well, you know enough already," she said, turning away.

Michael stopped her simply by laying his fingers on her shoulder. He realized she'd cooperated with him only because she feared he'd cause another scene in a bar that had finally settled down, and he felt a little bit guilty for being so pushy that he'd intimidated her.

Then she scorched him with a look that could have melted snow. He smiled at her, slowly pulling his hand away from her shoulder. She certainly didn't like anyone touching her. "Stash isn't paying one bit of attention to you," he said, deliberately putting his hand in his pocket so he wouldn't be tempted to use it again. "In fact, he's ignoring you. So, just answer one more question."

She sighed.

He assumed that was an assent of sorts. "Don't take this the wrong way, but you look old enough to have worked for Barnhart Steel long enough that these men would have accepted your position."

"They had, until I bought the bar," she explained in a tone of voice that said he should have figured that out for himself. "Their home away from home, their club, their haven. Understand?"

"Ohhh." He smiled wryly. "I'm surprised they still come here."

"There's nowhere else to go."

She faced Stash again. "Are you about finished?" she asked nicely. "I've got to get up early tomorrow so I can help Mom do the cooking for the anniversary party tomorrow night."

Stash tossed a half-eaten chicken leg to his plate. "Yeah, I'm done."

"I didn't mean you had to be done now. I just...just finish, okay?"

"Is that an order?"

Caitlin took a deep breath and shook her head sadly. New questions started forming in Michael's head. He glanced around, noting that not another man in the room seemed to be annoyed or distressed by Caitlin's presence. Then he looked at Stash again and realized the kid was more embarrassed than mad.

Michael held back a groan. Now he was getting the picture. There was nothing newsworthy about this bar or even the displaced steelworkers who were the regular patrons, but there weren't many sisters who loved their brothers enough to literally buy them a place to work. Yet that's exactly what Caitlin had done. That's the odd thing that Kiki had sensed but couldn't quite figure out. And that was a human interest story...the kind of human interest story that could be the lead for the Sunday magazine. In fact, it had the potential to be a series.

Michael watched Caitlin search out dishes from beneath the bar. She stacked them, then slid the stack across the counter at a point close to the door. She owned this bar. She worked for a *Fortune 500* company. She was quiet but not timid. Beautiful but not showy. And more concerned about taking her mother's dishes home then spending twenty minutes in an all-male bar where she wasn't really wanted.

Intrigued, Michael studied Caitlin as she slipped into her coat and hooked all the buttons, occasionally peeking at her brother with hopeful smiles. She was pretty as a sun-ripened peach and feminine, yet there wasn't a man in the room who would cross her. Even Bear had asked for her permission before taking aim at Michael. It was strange, in a good way, Michael supposed, but strange nonetheless. Maybe *Caitlin* should be the subject of the story, the beautiful no-nonsense woman who took care of her family.

Caitlin picked up the dishes and turned to leave but spun around again. "Oh, Bear, I almost forgot," she called down the bar to her cousin. "Mom said to remind you and your parents about the anniversary party tomorrow night."

"Again?" Bear groaned.

Without warning her grin was back. The wicked pixie grin that knocked Michael for a loop and made him want to kiss those lips. He had the strangest feelings for her. Just when he thought he knew enough about her, something made him curious to discover more. And not just for the story.

"Tomorrow night at seven," Caitlin said, then turned toward the door. "Don't make smart cracks, just be there."

Oh, I will be, Michael thought. For another chance to spend time with Caitlin, even finagling an invitation from surly Stash seemed possible. *Come hell or high water, I will be.*

Two

Caitlin, you're slicing that ham way too thin. Your dad likes it big and thick."

Caitlin silenced her mother with a mutinous glare. Frustrated, Colleen Petrunak raised her hands in despair. Her red hair and green eyes easily told her Irish heritage, but the way she held her temper with her stubborn family was a practiced art. "Is there ever going to be peace in this house?"

Carefully positioning the knife, Caitlin cut a whisper-thin piece of ham. "I don't know. You tell me."

Colleen shook her head and walked toward the oven. Though the kitchen was big and airy, the day's baking made it suffocatingly hot. Still it smelled wonderful. Assorted pies dotted one long counter. *Halusky*, pirogi and *holubky* warmed in big electric roasters by every outlet. Muffled conversations and laughter of the party guests drifted into the kitchen, making the day seem like Christmas or Thanksgiving, rather than the third of November.

"That pie has another ten minutes," Caitlin said, pushing damp tendrils of hair from her face. After all the cooking, she was sticky and tired and knew she should probably change, but considering the crowd was made up of people who'd seen her dirtier and sweatier, Caitlin opted to help her mother. Unless she volunteered to see this through to the bitter end, her mother would spend her anniversary party in the kitchen.

Colleen sighed. "Your dad hates brown crust."

"Dan can't eat ten pies." Heat and exhaustion had made Caitlin grumpy, but being angry with her father was her real problem tonight. And try as she might, she couldn't control her temper.

Though Colleen understood, she raised her eyes to the heavens. "Here we go again."

"Women weren't put on this planet to please men, Mom," Caitlin said, ignoring her mother's sigh. "You're a person with a brain, too. I think—"

"I think you should let me out of this!" Colleen said in a singsong voice, using her own brand of diplomacy. "Just because you're mad at your dad doesn't mean I have—"

"To be mad at him, too," Caitlin finished for her mother, spitefully slivering the ham again. "You always say that," she said tiredly. "But the simple truth is, Mom, I know you agree with me."

"Whether or not I agree with you has nothing to do with this."

Caitlin stopped cutting. "It has everything to do with this!" she said, staring at her mother incredulously. "Mom! Stash has been miserable for years! You have to see that."

"I do."

"And you should also realize that he's been less edgy, less grouchy, over the past few months."

Colleen sighed. "I have."

"Then it should make you just as mad as me that the minute I got him on the right track, Dad stirred everything up again."

"It does."

"So, if you'd speak up just this once—"

"There'd be a war." This time Colleen finished for her daughter. "You know that." Grabbing a pot holder, Colleen fished the last of the pies out of the oven. She looked at its pale crust and sighed.

Caitlin shook her head. "This is absurd!" she said, sweeping a hand in the direction of the sad-looking pie. "Everything, absolutely everything you do, is for Dad! You made ten pies. Ten pies," she repeated incredulously. "And every one of them is undercooked. He rules you!"

"I think you're overstepping your boundaries again, young lady."

Caitlin scampered around the simple wooden table. "How can I help it?" she pleaded. "What he's doing to Stash infuriates me!"

"Obviously," her mother deadpanned.

Realizing she was yelling at the innocent party, Caitlin deflated. "I'm sorry," she muttered, disgusted with her dad but more so with herself for losing her temper. "It took me two years to convince

Stash to go to college and that stupid contract had to pick his first semester to expire!''

Colleen deflated, too. "Yeah, I know. Rotten luck, huh?''

"One year,'' Caitlin said as she turned on the tap to rinse her hands. "If Stash had had one year in college before that contract expired, I know he wouldn't even have considered dropping out.''

"Look on the bright side, Cait,'' her mother commiserated. "He is only considering. He hasn't dropped out yet.''

"But he will,'' Caitlin lamented. She balled her hands into fists. "This is so frustrating! I know the company only promised to bring back the laid-off steelworkers to get the contract ratified, but Stash keeps saying where there's smoke, there's fire. He's sure that if they don't agree to the concessions the company will be forced to reinstate their old salaries as well as give everybody their job back. He heard some damned rumor about a big order that had to be filled and nothing I say will make him listen to reason.''

"And your dad doesn't help much,'' Colleen reluctantly admitted.

"Well, his tactics wouldn't be so effective if you didn't agree with him all the time,'' Caitlin quietly said.

Colleen gasped. "Cait, I *don't* agree with him.''

"You know that and I know that, but Stash doesn't know that. To him, your saying nothing is as good as agreeing.''

"I can't...I just...if I'd...''

"I know," Caitlin said with a sigh. "If you side against Dad, he'll be furious."

Her mother stiffened. "Cait, I really wish you wouldn't talk about your father like this. He loves Stash, too. Believe it or not, he's trying to point him in the direction he thinks is right."

Hearing the hurt in her mother's voice, Caitlin relented. "I know," she mumbled contritely. Caitlin knew that she was doing this all wrong. The way to win her mother's help was not by taking potshots at her father. Unfortunately, despite the fact that he was a good husband and a good father, Stan Petrunak, Sr. was strictly from the dark ages. He thought progress was a dirty word and there was no telling him otherwise.

"I'm going to start putting things on the buffet."

"No, Mom, I'll do it," Caitlin said. "This is your party, too. You should be greeting guests at the door." She eyed her mother's sweaty face and floury skirt. "I know, I'll hold everybody at bay for the next twenty minutes so you can go upstairs and put on something pretty."

"I would like to put on my good blue dress, the one you got me for Christmas last year, but your father—"

"I know, Dad doesn't trust me." Frustrated again, she started to bluster. "He hates my cooking. Hates the way I arrange the table. Hates my hair, my occupation. He won't let me do his taxes because all accountants are crooked. Need I go on?"

Colleen sighed heavily and shook her head. "All I wanted to do was set the table."

Caitlin sighed, too. "I'll do it," she insisted softly but firmly. "You run upstairs and put on your blue dress and I promise I'll arrange everything exactly the way you always do. No arguments. No trouble."

Chuckling in the way only mothers do when they're in the middle of a family feud, Colleen walked to the door, then paused. "Exactly how I always arrange things?" she asked skeptically.

"You have my word."

"No funny business?"

Caitlin grinned. "I promise."

"No salad forks?"

"I swear to God, I'll be the only person at the party to use one. And I'll do it in the kitchen, where I won't embarrass anybody."

Even as Caitlin was answering, Colleen pushed open the swinging door and bumped it into Michael Flannery. "Oh, pardon me! I'm so sorry." Flustered, she stepped back and let him enter the piping-hot kitchen.

"No harm done," Michael assured her, smiling at the older version of Caitlin. Though the woman was heavier and had short curly hair, she was undoubtedly Caitlin's mother.

"If you'll excuse me," Colleen stuttered, glancing down at her flour-covered skirt. "I'm going to change." She smiled once, then slipped through the door.

The appearance of last night's troublemaker had Caitlin's temper flaring again. With a stubborn father, a docile mother and a confused brother, *he* was the last person she wanted to see right now. "What are you doing here?"

Michael strolled into the room, inhaling all the way. "Stash invited me."

Turning away from him, Caitlin began to laugh. "Never in a million years. After last night, Stash would probably rather punch you than look at you."

"Yeah, well, I kind of thought that, too, so I didn't try to win Stash over right away. I started out by making friends with your cousin Bear."

She moved to another counter. "Mmm-hmm. I'll bet."

"We had a few beers, played a few games of poker on the machine and then he went home."

"I wish *you* would have," Caitlin mumbled, stirring the *halusky*.

"So then I sat at the bar again. And that's when I got smart. I asked for a cola, rather than a beer. I honestly wanted a cola, because I never drive drunk, but it was the perfect thing to order from your brother because it got the old conversation going between us."

"How lucky for you."

"I thought so," Michael agreed, leaning against the counter across the room from her. "Just goes to show you that it really is smarter to drink cola than liquor. Anyway, once I had him talking, I swooped in for the kill. I told him I thought you were cute and I insinuated I could keep you out of his hair tonight and maybe for a couple other nights if you were as nice as you are pretty."

"Huh! I'm surprised he didn't laugh in your face."

"Come to think of it, I am, too. But he didn't laugh. In fact, he seemed happy to invite me."

"I'll bet."

"He was," Michael insisted, leaning down to sniff the aroma coming from a roaster. "He said something about me sitting between you and your father. Introduced me to him a few minutes ago. Nice old guy. I can't think of a better spot at the dinner table. Right between a pretty girl and a man who loves to tell stories."

Caitlin threw her head back in frustration. "Great! Just great!"

"I thought it was great," Michael agreed, grinning because she was so mad. "In fact, I think I'm just about the luckiest guy in the city tonight." And he did. Not only was he about to be treated to a feast, but seeing Caitlin at her worst was pure pleasure—even better than seeing her all dressed up, as he'd expected. She was fire-spitting mad, her hair was in a state of disorder unparalleled by any hair he'd ever seen, and her jeans were that well-worn, tight kind he loved on a woman with hips like hers. If she could look this good after a day of cooking, cleaned up she'd probably knock men's eyes out of their heads.

"Get out of here," Caitlin grumbled, grabbing the knife with deadly intent. "I've got work to do."

"I'll help you," Michael decided on the spot. Ten minutes of casual conversation with Stan Senior, who insisted everybody call him Dad, had temporarily cooled Michael's interest in the bar. Stan Senior hated Catz and wished Caitlin had never bought it, which eliminated the softhearted sister story. So, considering that the night was young and it was a party, he'd gone in search of Caitlin. Now he'd have some fun.

"I don't want your help," Caitlin muttered. "I don't need your help."

"Oh, really?" Michael queried, jutting his chin toward one of three roasters. "Can you lift those?"

Caitlin's gaze slid the length of his tweed sport jacket and perfectly pressed gray trousers. "Can you?"

"Absolutely."

"Well, pretend I'm from Missouri. Show me."

In three strides Michael was across the room and grabbing a roaster. "Where to?"

"Dining room," Caitlin replied, trying hard not to be impressed. Men who dressed like Michael shouldn't be able to lift a roaster full of food. But he was big—not just tall but filled out. He was strong underneath what her father would call sissy duds. She nodded in the direction of the door. "I'll guide you the first time. After that you're on your own."

Michael smiled his agreement and followed her through the swinging door and down the wallpapered hall, which ran from the kitchen to the front door and actually divided the downstairs in two. On one side was a living room packed with gabbing people. On the other was the empty dining room. Huge parallel archways gave the effect of one big room, but as if observing some kind of rule, no one ventured past the hall.

Feeling oddly welcome, despite Caitlin's continued silence, Michael studied the surroundings. The entire house was as neat as a pin, but the decor was from the fifties. It was fussy but in an unextravagant way. Walls of pictures spoke of treasured memories and long-held traditions. Though he wouldn't want to live there, Michael had to admit he liked the place. In fact, the whole scene, gabby relatives and delicious aromas, reminded him of the party at his grandmother's house the Christmas before she died. Though that was over five years ago, he remembered her warm, welcoming house as though it was yesterday.

"Incidentally, Giorgio Armani," Caitlin tossed over her shoulder, "the dress tonight was casual."

Michael glanced at the sleeve of his tweed jacket. He was about to explain that he wasn't exactly sure what to wear, then decided to dish out as good as he got. "Really?" he asked, smiling innocently, even though he glanced meaningfully at her preteen attire. "I thought everybody was in their Sunday best."

Pointing at the long, thin buffet of a well-used walnut dining room set, Caitlin stifled her giggle. His sincere brown eyes and ingenuous smile were enough to weaken her knees, and when he teased her she was tempted to like him again. She had absolutely no idea why he had talked Stash into inviting him to their parents' anniversary party and even less idea why he'd teased her. She didn't trust him at all. In the first place, he'd asked too many questions the night before, and she got the feeling he was well practiced in using his considerable charm to get information. But what kind of information would he possibly want from a retired steelworker, a laid-off steelworker and a CPA for the steel company?

She peeked across the table to look at him as he turned to glance at her. For a moment they stared at each other. His eyes were dark and penetrating; hers were frankly curious. Then, in perfect harmony, their gazes moved downward. She scanned broad shoulders, trim hips. He looked his fill at her flour-covered sweatshirt.

She glanced at his big masculine hands. His long, lean fingers were wrapped around pot holders.

He admired her dipped waist and the very feminine look her body gave plain blue denim, before returning his attention to her face. Full, pouty mouth, pert little nose dusted with freckles, jeweled eyes.

Her gaze crawled up his sleeve, collided with biceps straining with the effort to hold a heavy roaster, then traveled across the glorious expanse of chest above the roaster.

Too impressed to be confused, Caitlin raised her eyes to catch his again. Across the empty dining room table earthy, basic attraction thumped between them. A hunger, sweet and unmistakable, swelled in Caitlin's breast, causing her eyes to widen in horror. Dear heaven, she had to get away from him! The very last thing she needed right now was to be attracted to a man—especially a man as persistent as this one.

When Caitlin ran out of the room, Michael quickly placed the roaster on the buffet and followed her, watching as she scurried to get away from him. The gentle, unaffected sway of her hips put a silly grin on his face. How long, he wondered, had it been since he'd met a woman who'd attracted him so quickly, so totally? And why did this one? She slipped through the kitchen door and let it slam into his stomach.

"What next?" he asked, not about to be deterred by her attitude. He knew that she was still upset about what had happened at the bar. But it was a little too soon to get into apologies or explanations. A smart reporter didn't ask permission to write a story unless he was sure he had one to write. That way, if the situation didn't pan out, he could disappear into the sunset and nobody's feelings would be bruised.

"Take one of the other roasters," Caitlin replied, dragging in a deep drink of air. Any other time it wouldn't have mattered one way or another how she looked, but suddenly she felt like a street waif. Even worse, if she as much as combed her hair, he'd think she'd done it to impress him. Unfortunately that would be true, because she didn't appreciate the thought that anyone who wasn't family would see her like this.

Michael hefted the second roaster as Caitlin busied herself with silverware. She tossed handfuls onto a cookie sheet, which acted as a makeshift tray. Even though she wouldn't look up at him, she wasn't scowling, just frowning. "If you follow me, I'll hold the door while you pass," he offered hopefully.

"If you don't wait for me, you can have that in the dining room before I'm even through gathering the flatware."

She raised her eyes as she spoke and it happened again. Amid the noise and confusion of a houseful of guests, something deep and profound arced between them. Stronger than sexual awareness, better than mutual appreciation, it was some kind of instinctive satisfaction that didn't have rhyme or reason. Flustered, Caitlin looked away. Equally stunned, Michael backed out of the kitchen. Physical attraction was one thing, but this crazy flapping of his heart was quite another. The last time he felt like this he almost got married.... Married? Maybe it was time to get back to Stash.

When the second roaster was nestled beside the first, Michael returned for the third but didn't say a word. As he left the kitchen, Caitlin breathed an enormous sigh of relief but held her ground about combing her hair. He'd grilled her and riled her the night before, and he'd deliberately poked and prodded until Stash was upset with her. This man was every bit as guilty as her father for Stash's foul mood, and Caitlin decided she'd do well to remember that. Whoever he was and whatever he wanted, it was trouble—and so was he!

On one of her frequent trips between the kitchen and dining room, Caitlin heard her mother announce that supper was served. She darted in the kitchen one last time, this time to pray she could hold her temper with her father. With that troublemaker here to add to the confusion, Caitlin knew that wasn't going to be easy. She dusted the flour from her sweatshirt, raked her fingers through her hair and then reluctantly made her way to the dining room.

At the huge parallel archway, Caitlin stopped and looked left at the living room full of people balancing plates on their knees, then right at the nearly filled dining room table and the stragglers at the buffet behind it. No sign of the stranger. Relief rippled through her. Maybe he'd gone home?

"Over here, Cait," Stan Senior called, waving a fork. He was in his early sixties, pudgy and ruddy-faced. "Saved ya a seat," he announced, then turned to his right. Caitlin's eyes got enormous with fury and fright when she saw her father direct his next comment to the stranger. Just as he'd said, he was to be seated right between her and her father.

"The family sits together for things like this," Stan Senior said as Caitlin glanced at Stash and noticed his face was red from holding back an ocean of laughter. Before the night was over, he'd get his. But she'd have to be subtle. If her father caught wind of the dissension in the ranks, he'd take full advantage and the war would be over before any real battles were fought.

"Grab a plate, dear," Colleen beckoned over her shoulder. "And hurry. We haven't even said grace yet."

So, they were down to guilt. Caitlin and her father hadn't been in the same room for two minutes and already her mother was bringing out the big guns. She took a deep fortifying breath, marched into the room and proceeded to fill a plate with the rich, buttery foods she'd spent all day helping to prepare. The sweet aromas prompted her stomach to growl.

"Here, let me help you with that."

Even without turning around, Caitlin knew who stood behind her. She'd know that voice in Grand Central Station, but the scent of after-shave—not musky, just woodsy and clean—was totally unexpected. Feathery whispers of feminine appreciation danced down her spine. She stiffened. "I'm strong enough to carry my own plate."

"Nonsense, I'll—" Michael began, but Stan, Sr. cut him off.

"Sit, sit, Michael," Dad blustered. "Don't be botherin' yourself with manners. We're all family here."

Michael scraped his chair away from the table but didn't sit. "That's funny," he remarked, smiling wryly. "My grandmother used to say something like

manners weren't just for company, they were for
family, too.''

Caitlin turned from the buffet and he held out her
chair. The gesture, though small and insignificant,
made her heart flutter, not because he was treating her
like a lady but because he was making a statement to
Dad—subtly standing up to him. For an instant Caitlin found herself wavering. It was hard to dislike this
guy.

Grace was brief and succinct. The last "amen"
hadn't sounded before forks and knives were clank-
ing. Laughter and gaiety filled the downstairs. Caitlin
sneaked a peek at Michael. *Michael.* She twisted the
name around in her head as she studied his profile and
decided she liked it. It was a no-frills name for a no-
frills man. He had money—that was obvious by his
clothes—but he didn't flaunt it. And he also didn't
mind being in a houseful of her boisterous relatives at
feeding time. In fact, he looked as though he was
having the time of his life.

"Ain't that right, Cait?"

Hearing her name, Caitlin first suffused with heat,
then shook her head to clear the haze. "I'm sorry, I
didn't hear you."

Dad slapped his fork beside his plate. "I said it's a
damned shame the way the economy's goin'."

Caitlin casually grabbed a homemade roll. She
ripped it in two and started to butter it. Choose your
words carefully, she reminded herself. Stay calm. Not
only do we have company of undetermined origin, but
you made a promise to your mother.

"Dad," she began reluctantly.

Intrigued by the hesitancy in her voice, Michael shifted to face her. To any onlooker it would seem all her concentration was on her roll, but Michael could almost see wheels turning behind troubled green eyes. She's beautiful, Michael thought once again. Beautiful and emotional and smart enough to be unconcerned about the first, even as she took great pains to control the second.

"The areas worst hit by this recession are steel and coal towns. You only have to travel as far as Virginia to find good work."

"Poppycock," Dad muttered, scowling. "Ask Michael here. He'll tell ya. The whole country's down...and why? Because them Republicans are hellbent on destroying the union."

"Dad!"

"Stan!"

Caitlin yelped, but her mother pleaded. Cait saw her mother glance in Michael's direction as if to caution her husband to watch his tongue until he was certain of his company.

"Sorry, boy," Dad sputtered, once again grabbing his fork. "It's a sore spot with me and I preach," he admitted, though without an ounce of repentance. "But it's the only way to get anything done."

"It's all right, Mr—"

"I've said we're not exactly what you'd call formal around here, boy. So call me Dad."

"It's all right, Dad," Michael repeated with a chuckle, liking this guy more by the minute. With so much apathy in today's world it was always interesting to find somebody who not only had opinions but had the courage of his convictions, as well. "I don't care one way or another about either political party. I'm independent."

Dad's eyes narrowed. "Oh, you're in that other party."

This time Michael shook his head as he laughed. "No. I have no affiliation."

"'Bout time you got some," Dad decided boisterously. "That's the way Stash always was until he ran nose first into a brick wall. Now he ain't so dumb no more."

Stash squirmed uncomfortably. "Dad, I was always in the union. And just because I voted for the concessions in the last contract—"

"It's people like you," Dad announced, interrupting his son, "who broke us. And people like you who gotta build us back up again." He glared once at his son as if gauging his next words. "You know that now, don't you? You know that you owe something and even if you don't benefit, you gotta stand behind these guys."

"Until the end of time, I will rue the day I bought that damned bar."

Caitlin's comment was muttered through clenched teeth and not nearly loud enough for Dad to hear, but Michael heard it. And used it. The story was forming in his head once again, less clearly but there nonetheless.

"You want your son to sort of campaign from Catz?" Michael asked Dad. "I thought you hated that bar."

Dad grinned wickedly. "Not always. With that location, he could get a crack at everybody going into or coming out of the mill. He could remind them of how everybody got laid off the last time they agreed to concessions.''

''For fifty cents I'd sell that place to the Women's Temperance Union and pray that they burned it down.''

Michael's lips twitched because he recognized that Caitlin's intended purpose for buying the bar must have backfired. Getting caught in a web of her own making obviously angered her mightily. But again he pretended he hadn't heard. ''Even though Stash gets nothing for this, you want him to crusade?''

''He'll get something,'' Dad snapped. ''He'll get the satisfaction of helping his friends.'' He glared at Stash. ''People he led astray.'' He looked at Michael. ''And maybe even earn himself a job in the union for his trouble.''

Caitlin made a gurgly sound of disgust in her throat, but Michael's attention was caught by the way Stash grinned. He tilted his head in question. ''You'd like that?'' he observed thoughtfully, even as yet another story outline formed in his mind.

''What Stash would like,'' Caitlin informed Michael curtly, ''is to be an attorney. Since he was twelve—''

Dad pounded a hand on the table. ''Don't you start again, missy!'' he thundered. ''He's got almost four years of college and three years in law school before he gets that damned degree you're pushing him into. And what would he do with all that schoolin', anyway? Nobody in this town can afford an attorney anymore!''

Caitlin started shaking. Remembering the butter knife beside her plate, Michael wondered if he shouldn't take cover.

"He could leave," she stated through clenched teeth. "The sun doesn't rise and set on Riverside! At least not on *this* side of the river." Her angry gaze caught Michael's jacket and inspiration struck. "Ask him," she suggested, thrusting a thumb in Michael's direction. "He'll tell you there's life across the river. Hell, there's prosperity across the river."

"You watch your tongue, young lady!" Dad yelped. "And don't you start tellin' me about jobs across the river. You coulda had three. Three." He leaned toward his daughter. "But you took the one right here," he reminded her, shaking a finger at her nose. "The one close to your ma, you said. Or was that a lie?"

Caitlin bounced from her chair and Michael caught it as it teetered precariously. "Why don't you say it?" she demanded indignantly. "For the past six years you've been hinting. Why don't you come right out and call me a company spy and get it over with!"

Even though a drama was being carried out at the head of the table, no one else seemed to notice, perhaps because the bulk of the crowd was now gathered in the living room and on the steps in the hall. Still, Michael held his breath.

Miraculously, Dad deflated. "Sit down, Cait," he muttered, glancing guiltily at his wife. "I know you took that job because you didn't want to live across the river." He drew a deep draft of air as Caitlin stood waiting. "I know you ain't in cahoots with the company. But dammit to hell! The way you keep pushing Stash out of town—"

Caitlin laid a hand on her father's arm. "I'm not pushing him out of town," she stated softly. "I just want him to go back to school and stay there. I bought Catz so he could work nights and go to school full-time and now you're—"

Stash threw his napkin beside his plate and rose. "Stop it, both of you! I'm sick of this! I get union from you and law school from you," he said, pointing from father to daughter. "And not once has anybody asked me what the hell *I* want to do. Dammit! I'm twenty-three years old! For God's sake, let me make up my own mind!"

Good for you! Michael thought, his respect for Stash growing. When Stash took his seat again, Michael's respect grew into admiration.

"Now, not another word. Not ever. Not again. Mother, this is the best *holubky* you've ever made."

"This *is* wonderful, Mrs. Petrunak," Michael rejoined, grateful for the chance to change the subject. He finally had his story. Concessions were old news, but how one displaced steelworker battled family, traditions and the odds to start over again seemed like just the right mixture of realism and sentiment to sell Sunday papers. He'd fill Kiki in because she'd found Catz, but he was doing the writing. There was a touchy situation here and he didn't trust it to anybody else.

Through his peripheral vision, Michael watched Caitlin pick at her food. Her guilty glance at her mother, which brought a sad frown, made her redden slightly. In another second, Michael watched Colleen scold Dad the same way, and he just barely held back a laugh. This family was loving and concerned but so stubborn and cocksure they somehow missed the obvious. He couldn't hold it against Dad. The man was fighting for tradition. He couldn't hold it against Caitlin; her arguments were too good. The sad truth was they were both right. There was no way to make peace here without a certified diplomat—or Mrs. Petrunak.

Caitlin slowly looked up. Her gaze skittered in the direction of her mother and then over to her dad. "How's the wood shop going?"

Dad cleared his throat. "Fine," he mumbled contritely. "Every retired man needs a hobby. How's the cat?"

"Ernest is fine, too. Cute. Fat." She laughed lightly. "That cat eats everything that isn't tied down!"

"I told ya to get a dog—"

"Oh, Dad, they're worse!" Stash chortled. "You remember that Lab we had? What was his name... Casey? That's it, Casey." He shook his head and laughed. "Ate your hunting boots, if I remember correctly."

Dad scowled appealingly. "Damned mutt! Ate your bucket, too, didn't he, Mother?"

"That he did! Ate your briefcase, right, Caitlin?"

"And Stash's Frisbee—"

"And two of my baseballs! You ever have a dog, Michael?"

"Uh, no," Michael admitted, suddenly feeling deprived. He'd missed out on family fights that ended in this wonderful contrition. He'd missed out on noisy dinners. He'd missed out on dogs.

"Why not?" Caitlin asked, leaning her elbow on the table so she could rest her cheek on her closed fist as she spoke directly to Michael. She smiled at him, welcoming him for the first time.

Michael's heart slammed against his ribs. When she smiled, her entire face lit up. With all that wild red hair she took on a timeless beauty that would have stopped him cold if her honesty hadn't already captivated him. She had the appeal of a person who stood up for what she believed in, without holding a grudge, without losing respect for her opponent, who in this case was her father. She was a smart, beautiful woman with real emotions, a refreshing change from the glossy sophisticates who haunted him, a breath of fresh air to a man whose life had settled into a predictably dull routine. And she was smiling at him.

Trying to be casual, he cleared his throat. "My parents didn't approve."

Dad wasn't about to let that slide by. "Now, there's a good boy. Listens to his parents."

Still facing Michael, Caitlin closed her eyes and sucked in her breath. Stash sighed eloquently.

"Dad, I'm—"

Dad waved a hand. "I know, I know. I'm butting out. But I still think you've got loyalties to consider."

"There's more than one way for Stash to help his friends," Michael interjected thoughtfully. "In fact, I have a friend I'd like him to speak with. A counselor."

"A counselor!" Dad bellowed. "My son's not—"

Before Dad could gain steam and momentum, Michael interrupted him. "An *employment* counselor," he qualified. "Somebody who'll help Stash figure out the kind of work that suits him and then help him to find a job that fits into that category." He could see the story now. He'd pick it up right from Stash's first visit to the counselor and go from there.

Stash immediately warmed to the idea. "Really?" he asked excitedly. "I mean, I'm not a hardship case or anything. I have a job," he reminded Michael as he glanced at Caitlin. "And I have money saved so I can pay."

"Let's not worry about that part just yet," Michael said as he took a pad from his breast pocket and began jotting down the counselor's name. "Go see Myranda on Monday. Give her all the facts and let her give you your options."

Even as he was speaking the doorbell chimed. "Get that, will you, Cait?" Colleen requested with a soft smile.

Swallowing, Caitlin nodded. Maybe it was best for her to get out of the room. Two more minutes and she'd be choking that man. Stash knew what he wanted. He wanted to be an attorney. He was wavering only because their father was pushing. She rose and scooted around chairs and between people. If this Michael character sent her brother to some counselor, she'd undoubtedly convince him that seven years of school was just too many and before you know it Stash would be sweeping the streets or picking up garbage.

Caitlin did a slow burn. Michael might be good-looking and have impeccable manners, but he riled her constantly. He was always poking his nose into their business, first asking questions, now giving advice. Why couldn't he just leave them alone?

She yanked open the door and faced the strangest-looking creature on God's green earth. The woman's flared denim skirt nearly reached the porch and she wore enough jewelry to start her own store.

Belatedly remembering her manners, Caitlin asked, "Can I help you?"

The young woman scratched her fingers through her ear-length bob, which was plastered with something that made the curls cling as though still wet. "This Stan Petrunak's house?" she asked.

Caitlin stepped back. "Yes."

"Is Michael Flannery here?"

"No. Well, maybe. Is he tall—"

"Good-looking and dressed like a doctor? Yeah, that's him."

Nonplussed, Caitlin stared. The Gypsy pushed horn-rimmed glasses up on her nose. "Is he ready to go yet?"

Caitlin smiled slowly. "He's ready."

"Tell him Kiki's waiting in the car, okay?"

"I'll tell him," Caitlin replied, malicious intent oozing through every word. She spun and ran into the dining room. "Michael, there's a Kiki at the door. She said to tell you she's waiting in her car."

Silently cursing as he smiled at his host, Michael rose. Damned impatient woman! She wanted the satisfaction of knowing she'd sniffed out a story. And to keep her out of the way, he had to lose precious research time. "I'm sorry to eat and run," he apologized guiltily. "But Kiki..." How did one explain Kiki? One couldn't. He slipped between the table and the buffet.

Even before he reached the hall, Caitlin tossed his coat to him.

"Will you please stay on your own side of the river!" she growled in a whisper. "My brother knows what he wants. He doesn't need your counselor. So just take your tailored suit and fancy ideas and get back on your own turf, where people don't mind paying a counselor to tell them what they already know."

Insulted to the tips of his toes, Michael drew a sharp breath and stepped back. He was trying to help and she was showing him the door, shoving his coat at him and in general acting like a spoiled child. He almost couldn't believe that the same woman who had dealt so rationally with her father could turn on him like a sixteen-year-old bully.

He grabbed her chin and forced her eyes to meet his. "You're every bit as shortsighted as your father and every bit as stubborn!"

He dropped her chin as if it burned him and stormed out of the house, cursing his hormones. The absolute softness of her skin had been so unexpected that he had almost disgraced himself by kissing her. Then, under the bright yellow light on her parents' front porch and in full view of her company, she would have cracked him a good one.

Three

The next morning, Caitlin awakened feeling the same way she did when she fell asleep: miserable. Not only had the touch of Michael's fingers tingled on her chin for what had seemed like an eternity, but his words had followed her home and crawled into bed with her. And so had the look in his eyes. Anger she could have handled. Scorn, contempt, would have been okay, too. But disappointment? She sensed that she'd failed him somehow, and as she drifted off to sleep she realized that she felt disappointed, too.

Confused, she rolled out of bed and slid into a soft raspberry-colored robe. She rubbed a hand over her face and then threaded her fingers through her tangled red hair. Her vision was fuzzy and so was her brain. Now what? she asked herself, padding to the bathroom.

It would be easy enough to find him and apologize for snipping at him. She *had* recognized his good breeding. She could admit it. She smelled the old money just as clearly as his woodsy after-shave. After a couple of calls to certain gossipy friends, she'd know how to find him. Then she could tell him she saw his point and that she'd let her twenty-three-year-old brother make up his own mind about what he wanted to do with the rest of his life.

Satisfied, she showered and then dressed in old jeans and an oversized sweatshirt. While coffee brewed, she let her orange cat, Ernest, out for his morning routine—whatever that was—and grabbed the Sunday paper from the bottom step of the long, narrow stairway that led to her apartment above Buzz Hanwell's garage. The stairwell was enclosed, but cold November air nipped her bare toes, and she was dancing when she reached the door of her apartment.

Eyeing the headlines she walked into the kitchen. Thumbing through the different sections of the paper, she poured a mug of coffee. Yanking out the TV listing, she got milk from her refrigerator. By the time her coffee was properly prepared, she was shuffling to find the city magazine that was lovingly enclosed in every Sunday edition.

She found it and grabbed her coffee at the same time. Sipping, she made her way into her living room. A coaster had a permanent home on her cherry-wood coffee table because she always drank her coffee in her bentwood rocker. Her black pumps lay drunkenly in front of her brown tweed sofa because she always wilted there at the end of the day. And her peach-rust-and-beige-flowered drapes were drawn open because she never wanted to miss what was going on out in the street. Sunday mornings it was quiet. Then again, so was she.

After a long, satisfying drink of liquid energy, Caitlin settled down to read. She loved this magazine because it mirrored what was happening in Riverside—and not just on the good side of the river. She flipped and skimmed, studied the article chronicling the life of the city's oldest resident and then decided she'd better get dressed for church.

She absently tossed the magazine beside her empty cup and headed for the bedroom. Twenty minutes later she reappeared looking all spit-and-polish, except that she was in her stocking feet because her black leather pumps were by the sofa. Her tailored black and pink tweed coat reached midcalf and had an accompanying pink wool scarf that accented its open neck. Had it snowed, she'd have proudly displayed her new black boots, but until it snowed, only sissies wore boots, except scrungy ones with jeans. Old habits died hard on this side of the river and dress-up boots weren't welcome. However, Caitlin had braved ridicule with a felt hat—a wide-brimmed black hat with a little pink accent feather. It was simple but elegant and sat squarely on top of her head. She could tuck her hair under it and look like royalty or leave her hair down and look like Caitlin. This side of the river wasn't ready for royalty, so Caitlin wisely let her red curls tumble to her shoulders. She slid into her shoes, pulled on black leather gloves and grabbed her purse from beside the magazine, *Flannery's Place*.

Michael *Flannery*?

As she turned back to the magazine, fury, confusion, and stupefaction tumbled through her. Michael Flannery! Sweet Lord! How could anybody in this city miss the connection? Old money and Flannery. In Riverside the two were synonymous.

Shock weakened her knees and she dropped to her rocker. Even as she picked up the magazine her eyes grew enormous with rage. A story! The idiot was sniffing for a story... Stash!

Anger put strength back in her knees and fire in her blood. She'd kill him! If he *dared* subject Stash to the further ridicule of being the object of some introspective piece of trash, she'd kill him!

Livid, she scrambled down the narrow stairway and to her car. She didn't feel the bite of the wind or smell the scent of the brewing storm. Fueled with anger and protective pride, she stomped on the gas and went.

Oh, she knew where he lived. Flannery Towers. Built, owned and managed by Flannery Enterprises. Sole possessor of Flannery Textiles, Flannery Development and Flannery Publications. Which put out *Riverside Times*, *Riverside This Month* and *Flannery's Place*. Her foot jammed the gas pedal to the floor. Oh, she'd been so stupid!

Her car had barely sputtered to a stop when she ground the gearshift into park and twisted the key. She opened the door and welcomed the cold rush of wind on her hot, angry face. Stomping, she made her way to the sparkling glass and chrome door of the luxurious brick building, but when she yanked it open, a doorman appeared.

"Miss?"

She stared at the man who was dressed like a member of the royal guard. Think, she commanded herself. Doormen were for screening guests. They usually didn't like angry ones. She pasted a smile on her face. "Hi! Guess you know who I'm here to see."

His gaze moved from her hat to her pumps. "Can't say that I do."

She brightened her smile and conjured a blush, managing to make herself look innocent and convincing all at the same time. "Mr. Flannery."

Turning away, the doorman dismissed her. "He's out."

The sea dog! How dare he be out when she wanted to lambaste him.

She scrambled after the doorman and tugged on his sleeve. On inspiration, she smiled sheepishly. Look like a long-lost lover, she commanded herself, and almost pulled it off. "Can you tell me where?" she asked hopefully.

The doorman's face scrunched in confusion. "Can't see why not. He's jogging." He turned and pointed at the glass. "Out there."

Out there was Riverside Park. It was the eighth wonder of the world, as far as Caitlin was concerned. Mated to the river, the park wove its way through the entire city, but on this side of the water it was fenced in by a high wrought-iron gate and that gate was guarded by two plaster of paris lion heads.

Puzzled, she turned back to the doorman. "Can I get in there?" she asked, seriously thinking one probably needed a key.

The doorman dismissed her again with a shrug and an impatient "Can't see why not."

Her anger started to bubble again. Not only was that twit Flannery about to announce her brother's plight to the entire city, but his doorman—and it was *his* doorman because he owned this damn building— had barely given her the time of day. Fury boiled and her chest started to heave again. Defiantly, she shook back her hair and marched across the quiet tree-lined street and to the lions.

"Don't you say a word!" she warned them as she tested the gate with a little push. It gave with no fur- ther persuasion. Once through the passage she glared at the iron door and left it open. Let somebody stew about that!

But in another minute, it was Caitlin who was stewing. A glance down the river showed the park was empty. The cold wind that whipped under her coat and thin dress told her why. She shivered. Couldn't he have gone to a health club like a normal person?

The wind caught her hat and her hands flew to anchor it. In that second, he appeared around a ga- zebo. Other sections of the park had benches and squirrels and picnic tables. This part had gazebos. She counted six. Idiots.

A bite of wind stung her legs. At least a hundred yards away he rhythmically approached her. She glanced down at her heels. If she sacrificed her favor- ite shoes and walked through the grass she could catch him, scream at him and get out of this wind. It was worth it.

Glaring, hanging on to her hat and fuming, she stomped ahead. If he saw her, he gave no indication. But his head was bent and there were plugs in his ears.

Those plugs were connected to a thin wire that ran to a little radio at his waist.

On she trudged, heels sticking and sinking. On he jogged, lithe and graceful. Though her gaze was angrily locked on his gray sweat suit, he never once glanced up.

Two steps from him and they were almost parallel.

Four clumsy stomps from her and she was in front of him. Still, he didn't look up. It was self-preservation when she slapped her palm onto his chest to keep him from running over her.

"What the..." he sputtered, nearly tumbling backward. "Oh, it's you."

"Yes, it's me," she sneered, putting her hands on her hips. "I finally put two and two together."

With Johnny Mathis crooning softly in his ear, Michael couldn't hear her but he could certainly see her. Under the wide brim of a cute hat, green eyes flashed with fire as her mouth went a hundred miles an hour. A pink scarf was nestled about her chin, accenting her delicate coloring and making her look warm and sophisticated at the same time. Her trim coat easily highlighted that sophistication. Gleaming hose caressed shapely calves, but her earth-covered heels made him frown again. She certainly must have been in a hurry to stomp through the grass rather than use the sidewalk.

He stretched one of his earphones from his ear. "You listen to me," she was yelping, and he let the plug snap into his ear again as he jogged in place to recapture his rhythm.

"I think I heard everything I want to hear from you last night," he announced, and didn't wait for her answer. Instead, he jogged around her, three jumps through the grass and then back onto the sidewalk.

A gust of wind pasted red and orange leaves to her legs. Outraged, Caitlin didn't feel them or the wind. She tugged on her hat and ran after him.

"Listen to me!" she shouted, and growled low in her throat when he kept right on jogging. "I won't let you run away, because I won't let you—" Her brow furrowed. He didn't stiffen, cock his head or even break stride. He couldn't hear her!

Red-hot Irish blood heated to its limits. Curvy legs scampered into action. When she reached him she grabbed one of his biceps. Taking advantage of the element of surprise, she easily spun him around. While he panted, she yanked the earplugs out of his ears.

"You pea brain!" she shrieked. "If you think I'm going to let you write a story about Stash—"

"Haven't you ever heard the old saying about honey and vinegar?" Michael asked, bending to retrieve the thin cord that dangled from his radio. He put the earphones back in his ears and off he went.

Completely aghast, Caitlin buzzed after him. But knowing he was being chased, Michael began to pick up the pace. She quickened her step, cursed her shoes and finally caught him by a latticework gazebo. Chest heaving, she stared at him while she caught her breath.

"My brother," she panted, "is very confused right now. You've got to understand that having another person poking into his life will do more harm than good...."

Once again, he could see but couldn't hear her. Her mouth was still moving but her eyes were serious and set upon his face as if begging for understanding. Her nose had reddened but the flush in her cheeks was a healthy compliment to her already beautiful skin. If the look on her face was any gauge, she did remember that you draw more flies with honey than vinegar. He at least owed her the courtesy of hearing her out. Even before he had his earplugs removed, she whapped his arm.

"Listen to me!"

"I will listen," he patiently enlightened her. "But I can't stop running. I have to keep my heart rate this high for another ten minutes." He jogged away but didn't replace the earphones.

She groaned in exasperation. "How can you hear me when you're jogging?"

"I can listen and run, too," he informed her over his shoulder. "If you want me to..."

When the wind stole the rest of his words and turned them into an inaudible muffle of baritone, Caitlin scrambled after him. "My brother is very confused," she explained, "because my father makes him feel like he single-handedly destroyed the union just because he voted for the concessions in the last contract." She paused and grimaced, though Michael didn't see. "He also talked all his friends into doing the same thing. Once the contract was ratified, everybody got laid off. The company never broke any promises. They didn't have to. Stash and his friends played right into their hands by assuming too much and taking ambiguous statements the wrong way."

The wind grabbed the short curls on the back of Michael's head and waved them upward. Caitlin watched the spectacle and tightened her hold on her hat. "Anyway, it took two years before the stink settled, but once it had, Stash was talking about going to college. For weeks I wheedled and cajoled and finally one day..."

Disoriented, she stopped talking. She'd subconsciously picked up Michael's rhythm, and that put him perfectly in her line of vision. When his back bobbed up, her eyes followed it. She saw muscle, sinew, sweat and a gray sweatshirt. It was a nice back, a great back, but a smart woman wouldn't watch it when she wanted to think. She lowered her eyes and her gaze collided with tight—

She had a choice: watch the scenery or get in front of him.

She cleared her throat and picked up the pace. "Anyway," she said, and her words misted in front of her. Her lungs started to burn from the cold and her nose began to run. She sniffed and grabbed her wool scarf. "I got him to enroll and everything was going great, but..." She passed Michael and turned to face him as she pressed the scarf to her face to protect her respiratory system. Diligently exercising, Michael never broke stride. Caught up in the spirit of things, Caitlin didn't slow down, either. In her trim coat and high heels she jogged backward and pleaded her brother's cause to a man who just gave her a silly grin. "The union contract ran out and everybody and their brother brought their comments into the bar." Tying the scarf at the back of her head, she went on, "I could tell Stash was trying to stay out of it, but he's got an undeniable rapport with his peers and my dad wanted him to use it to undo the damage caused by talking everybody into ratifying a bad contract the last time around."

She teetered once and Michael steadied her by the shoulders. Had she shouted or insisted he stop to talk with her, Michael would have refused. He would have happily spoken with her once his workout was complete, but her actions struck him in the oddest way. He was both amused and impressed that she'd brave the cold, jog backward and plead just to protect her brother. Loyalty didn't run any deeper than this, he decided with a grin, thinking that was the trait he liked best about her. He didn't really know this woman, yet he got strange compelling signals from her. It was almost as though everything she did, everything she said, held a deeper meaning. As if this one conflict had been created to reveal her entire personality, her convictions, her thoughts.

"So, what, exactly, did Dad do?" Michael asked, pointedly forcing his attention back to the conversation. In another ten feet they'd reach a gazebo and not only could they get out of the wind, but they'd have some privacy. Then he'd answer her allegations about his story because she deserved an honest discussion; but he also wanted to buy the time to try to figure out why she had this odd effect on him.

"Oh, little things," Caitlin replied, drawing in a deep draft of air when she realized he really was listening to her. Uneasily, she glanced behind her but the path was clear.

"What little things?"

Caitlin turned to face him again just as a snowflake hit his cheek and melted instantly. Fascinated, she stared at the tiny drop of water, then the day's growth of beard that darkened his cheeks and chin. It was amazing that this man could look sexy when he was warm from exertion and unshaven. Yet he did. He looked sexy and very male. This was Michael Flannery without artifice, without benefit of the possessions his money could buy. This was how he'd look first thing in the morning, still warm from the covers and sporting the evidence of twenty-four hours without shaving....

When she lifted her gaze to meet his brown eyes, he was watching her closely. He very definitely saw the way she had been studying him.

"Lots of stupid stuff," she muttered, suddenly feeling foolish. What was she doing staring at a strange man? Men were men. This one was no different than any other. There was no reason to stare. "Like making reference to how poorly paid some of the old steelworkers were now that they had to take other jobs. He talked about deprived kids and wives who now had to work and..."

Suddenly Michael grabbed her shoulders and stopped her. "What else?"

"Two people lost their homes because they couldn't make mortgage payments." Even as she spoke, he directed her up a step.

"That's not enough to change his mind or make him feel guilty."

"No," Caitlin admitted as he pushed her into darkness. Her chest was rising and falling dramatically, but exercise and cold had been joined by fear. "Where are we?"

"In a gazebo. Out of the wind."

She remembered the airy latticework and swallowed. "But it's dark in here."

"In the winter we line these with plywood to keep the snow out. The stuff's light, so you can't tell from the outside that the gazebos are lined. We don't want to spoil the effect."

Leave it to the rich, she thought sourly. "Oh."

He took a pace toward her.

She took a pace back.

"You were saying?"

After a deep, fortifying breath, she continued, "Once the stage was set, Dad dragged out the big guns. The last contract. He reminded Stash that he'd been the self-appointed leader who got them into this mess and told him that the only way out was with a strike—a *big* strike."

Michael sighed wearily. "It's way too late for that. The whole industry's in trouble. Your brother's not responsible for what happened here in Riverside any more than a big strike can solve the problems of an industry plagued by foreign imports."

Finally relieved, Caitlin sighed. "Thank you."

"You're welcome," he replied, stepping close again. He ran one finger along the top of her scarf, grazing her frozen nose in the process. Two of his fingers dipped beneath the lightweight wool and skimmed her lips.

"What are you going to do?" she asked, and neither one was sure if she was probing about his immediate questing or his article.

Realizing that he was touching her, becoming hypnotized by a magnetic pull he didn't quite understand, Michael pulled his hand back and paced to the other side of the gazebo, though that really wasn't all that far. Her scent filled the air, asking him to return to her, to touch her again, if only to make sure she was real.

He sighed, disgusted not with himself but with the situation. Why couldn't he have met her on the street, in a restaurant, through a business contact? Why did they have to be negotiating.

Finally he said, "I have a cousin Kiki who's a bit of a crackpot."

Caitlin cleared her throat. "I know. I met her."

"That's right. At your parents' party." He sighed. "Anyway, I feel the same way about Kiki as you feel about Stash."

"You're trying to get her life in order?"

He turned to face her then, even though he really couldn't see her in the darkness. At least, not from this distance. "Precisely. Kiki's a good kid with lots of potential. So much, in fact, that I'm doing everything in my power to keep her with Flannery Publications. But my dad can't seem to see past her gum snapping and her sticky hair."

Caitlin giggled and the sound echoed around him, softening the mood, bridging the gaps that seemed to exist between them.

Michael began to relax. "That's where your brother comes in."

"How could my brother possibly help your cousin?" she asked, the question dripping with skepticism.

"Kiki's positive there's a story behind this latest union controversy. At first I didn't agree, but now that I've met Stash I do."

"Oh, so what you're saying, then, is that you don't care if my brother gets hurt as long as your cousin writes her story."

"I'm writing this story."

"You're writing the story?" she asked, confused.

"I have to."

"You're losing me," she said, and just from the tone of her voice, Michael could tell he really was.

"*Flannery's Place* has a certain reputation to maintain, and if we print this story the wrong way we'll lose some of our credibility. I have to protect the company's reputation, even though I don't generally write for the magazine."

"You don't?"

"No. I write for the paper."

"Oh."

She paused for a minute and he didn't say anything while she thought about what he'd told her.

"You don't run the paper?"

He smiled. "Nope. My dad still runs everything."

"But Kiki's the magazine editor?"

"Yes."

"And your dad wants to can her?"

"Yes."

"Why don't you let him? Stash getting laid off from the mill was the best thing that ever happened to him. Maybe you shouldn't protect her."

"I have to. What my dad wants to do is wrong. He's not giving her enough of a chance to learn. He wanted her to be great the minute she took the chair behind the big oak desk, and she's not. But she's only nineteen—"

"Nineteen! And she runs a magazine?"

"The Sunday supplement to her family's newspaper. Not exactly *Vogue*."

"But still—"

Michael held up both hands to stop Caitlin's argument. "It was nepotism, pure, plain and simple, that got Kiki her job. But, to be frank, nobody else on staff wanted it. As it is, my dad's going to be recruiting from the university if he fires Kiki. And I don't think he should. Not only would that destroy her, but she really does have potential, drive and desire. The kid has desire like you wouldn't believe. I think she'll be great, given a little time."

"And a little help from you."

He sighed. "And a little help from me. Look, I know what you're thinking, but you're way off base. I'm not doing her job for her. I'm directing her. Showing her what my dad wants because he was too vague. When he called her in and yelled at her, all he said was the magazine was getting too fluffy. You know, too feminine."

"Really? I've never thought so."

"You haven't?" he asked, truly surprised.

"No. Not at all."

"I wish you'd talk to my dad."

She snickered. "What's the point? I'm a woman. He'd probably just remind me that as a woman I like fluff and femininity and that's why I like the magazine." Another minute passed in silence, then she said, "So how does one story—how does *this* story—help your cousin if you're writing it?"

"She found it."

"And that's enough?"

"For an editor that's everything. It proves she's beginning to understand the vision of the magazine my father has. She's discovered his focus. But the wrong writer could lose the point. That's what makes editing so tricky."

"If it's so tricky, why aren't you the editor?"

"I don't want to be."

"You want to be a reporter—a writer—the bottom of the newspaper barrel?"

"I like being a reporter. And as for being the bottom, that's relative. A matter of perspective." He grinned. "Especially when you're on the board of directors of the company that owns the newspaper."

"Hmm," she said, thinking again, and he let her. Then she sighed and brought the conversation back on track. "I still have no idea of what you could write about my brother."

He ran his hand across his chin, stalling for time because he really wasn't sure the story he wanted to write was about her brother. Most of the time, Caitlin emerged as the most colorful character in this scenario. The woman who bucked tradition to get her education, who worked in the mill's upper echelon, who remained in the neighborhood, close to her family despite the fact that she could afford to live uptown, and who jumped in to help her brother, fighting for him the same way she must have fought for herself when she wanted to go to college.

Still, Stash did have some interesting, not to mention universal troubles that would catch the senior Flannery's eye and probably gain another chance for Kiki. And he could always write a story about Caitlin later if he played his cards right.

"There are lots of fascinating things about your brother," Michael said once he'd made up his mind. "His problems, his peers and the mill contract coming home to him again. You just don't see the angles because you're too close to the situation."

"Maybe," she agreed, but she still hadn't dropped that note of skepticism from her voice.

"Trust me, Caitlin, there's a story here."

"Somehow I can't see anything about my brother making front page news."

"It wouldn't," he assured her, remembering that privacy was a part of the problem. "The story is human interest and possibly even self-help, if I structure this right."

"Structure what right?"

"The story, as I see it, is pertinent and necessary," he announced, feeling confident enough to walk over to her again. "If we can follow your brother's progress as he makes his way through the problems of putting himself into the work force again, we may show a couple of hundred other men how to do it, too."

"Oh," she said, with a sigh of understanding.

"If Stash tells the world—his world, those men who were laid off with him—that he went to an employment counselor, that she helped him find his talents and directed him to a school or college or wherever he needed to go to develop them, it's bound to have a domino effect."

"Could be," she said, then moved away from him.

"And seeing Myranda could only be good for Stash."

She turned. "He wants to be an attorney."

"If he really feels that strongly," Michael said, smiling slightly at her persistence, "then Myranda will probably direct him to go to law school."

Caitlin laughed. "I suppose you're right," she said, and walked over to stand in front of him. "You know you're not *all* bad. In fact, I'm beginning to see that we're a lot alike. At least in how we take care of our families."

He shook his head, chuckling because he couldn't believe how stubborn she was. No matter how subtly put she'd just disagreed with him, maybe even insulted him. "You still don't like the idea of a story, do you?"

"Not one bit," she said, although she laughed again. "But if I've learned nothing else from our conversation this morning, I've learned that you're a pretty nice guy. Maybe honest is a better word. You'd never force Stash to be a part of this if he didn't want to. So, I can relax because he's just a little too shy to let you and a camera crew follow him around the city. Come on, let's jog up to your apartment and get a cup of coffee."

For a few seconds, he stared at her, more disoriented than surprised. Never had he met anybody who could disagree with you completely, insult you subtly—and not so subtly—and still smile at you. "Did you know you're a hell of a lot like the weather?"

She frowned, then shivered. "If you're trying to offend me by calling me cold, it won't work. I've been called worse."

"No, I was referring to unpredictability."

"Unpredictability?" she echoed, confused. "I've never been called unpredictable. I'm the most consistent, logical person you'll ever meet."

"Consistent?" he asked, and started to laugh. "I might go along with the logical," he said, reaching down to undo her scarf. He pulled it away from her face and tucked the ends into her coat again. "But consistent? Never."

"Well, if you don't like the weather around here," she said, trying to keep the tone light, but there was a catch in her voice, almost a quiver, something akin to anticipation rather than nervousness. "Let me suggest you move to a warmer climate."

"Oh, no," he quickly contradicted, then he smiled. She was feeling it, too, whatever it was. Anticipation. Happiness. Something was in the air and it had them both a little too giddy to be spellbound but curious enough not to walk away even though they were talking nonsense. "Weather changes aren't necessarily bad. For instance, your temper reminds me of the wind—blustery and frigid but gone before you know it. And when it goes, it takes away all the bad feelings, all your anger. Then you smile and it's like the sun coming out again and whoever you were mad at is off the hook."

"I don't believe in holding a grudge," she muttered, sliding away from him.

"No, you don't," he agreed and took the step that brought them face-to-face again. "And that's good." He put his hands on her shoulders, mostly to keep her where she was but partially to see her reaction to his touch. She didn't move. She didn't even seem to breathe. And the world became quiet and still, almost as though he'd just made a plea for silence.

"Now, your hair's like the leaves. Red and sassy." As he said it, he threaded his fingers through the soft strands at her nape. "This is nice," he said, referring to her hat. "But I think we'll take it off." He grabbed the rim of her black felt hat and tipped it off her head, then gently tossed it across the three feet to the circular bench that was flush against the round wall of the gazebo.

He didn't see fear or questions in her eyes, only curiosity, a mirror image of what she undoubtedly saw in his. Again something seemed to sizzle between them, but this time he welcomed the magnetism, the pull, the warm intimacy that had no rhyme or reason, because they were alone, cocooned in their own little world. Whatever they did in these next few minutes would be private, secret, something they could keep to themselves for the rest of their lives.

"And your skin is so pale, so clean," he whispered. "It reminds me of newly fallen snow." Slowly, hypnotically, he caressed her cheeks with his thumbs. "From the minute you bellied up to the bar at Catz, I've wanted to kiss you. I don't know what it is about you, but you seem to fascinate me."

No man had ever said she was fascinating, and if any man had, undoubtedly her response would have been laughter. Today, with this man, she understood exactly what he was saying because she felt the same way about him: confused, interested, curious and somehow comfortable. But that was hardly a reason to kiss a man you didn't really know...was it?

She blinked up at him. He smiled slowly. The answer to her question didn't seem to matter, since he was obviously going to kiss her whether she wanted him to or not.

Knowing her protests would be futile, Caitlin stood perfectly still. He lowered his head and she closed her eyes, but it wasn't his lips she felt. Instead, his warm tongue traced a line from one corner of her mouth to the other. Her breath shuddered out on a sigh and she was suddenly grateful for the hands on her shoulders. That one sweep of his tongue had just liquefied her knees.

"What are you doing?" she whispered, though she didn't pull away.

He answered her whisper with a whisper. "I'm not sure."

Again his tongue slid from one corner to the other and swallowing, Caitlin opened her eyes. A kiss she could have handled, but this she had to stop.

"Michael..."

"Shh," he said, then softly pressed his lips to hers.

The kiss was light and sweet but somehow also abnormally sensual. He was reaching her on a level she didn't understand, on a level she didn't know existed, and it was every bit as frightening as it was exhilarating. She closed her eyes and willed herself not to melt into a puddle at his feet.

"Open your eyes, Cait."

"I can't." Her answer was something between a moan and a whisper, and hearing it Michael slid an arm around her waist.

"I want to see your eyes. I love your eyes."

Hearing the male need in his voice, Caitlin answered his plea, if only because she had to stop this. But before she could open her mouth to say anything, he kissed her again. Involuntarily, her eyes closed, but he didn't request that she open them; he just kept on kissing her. Slow and soft became inquisitive and curious, and inquisitive and curious became bold and adventurous, but when his tongue slipped into her mouth, adventurous became serious. A long-forgotten hunger sprang up inside her and she slipped her hands up the wall of his chest until she could clasp them around his neck and bring herself closer for more. Deeper and deeper he took her until somewhere in the realm of sanity a warning bell rang.

Breathless, Caitlin broke away. "Stop."

"Uh-uh. Too late," he said, then took her mouth again.

The momentum picked up as if they'd never stopped, and that really frightened her. She didn't know him well enough to kiss him this way, yet it didn't feel like a mistake or an accident. It felt absurdly natural.

She pulled away again and sucked in her breath. "Enough, okay?"

Michael rubbed a hand along the back of his neck. "Sorry," he mumbled, stretching to retrieve her hat. He plopped it on her head.

She took another deep, fortifying breath and glanced around until she saw the opening that was the door. Tiny white snowflakes were dancing on the breeze, reminding her that beyond the door lay sanity and reason.

Slowly she slid to the opening, not trusting herself to lift her feet from the floor. "I...think I'll take a rain check on the coffee."

He cleared his throat. "Yeah, sure."

Holding back a sigh of relief, she began to step through the portal. "Goodbye."

"Goodbye," he said, watching her. "I'll guess I'll see you when I come by to talk to Stash."

She stopped her foot in midair, just inches from stepping out of the gazebo and into the real world. If he wrote this story, even if he came around only to try to convince Stash to let him write the story, she'd see him again. He'd make sure of it and then she'd have to deal with this. "I really wish you wouldn't do that."

His brow furrowed. "Wouldn't do what?"

"Write about my brother."

"I thought we had this all settled?" he asked, sounding totally confused. "That you understood this was Stash's decision."

"It's not right," she said, forcing her voice to be as firm as it could be. "It's really not. Stash is very vulnerable because of the way my dad—"

"I think you're too hard on your dad, Caitlin," Michael interrupted. "He's harmless. My dad had the power to fire Kiki, but your dad really can't do anything to Stash. I mean, I know he blusters and bellows, but even if he wanted to, he couldn't really *do* anything. My dad can take Kiki's job away. And to make matters worse, Kiki's only nineteen. Stash is twenty-three. Old enough that your father can't even forbid him to drink in a bar, let alone..."

He paused, and though Caitlin suspected he was making certain connections that must have eluded him until now, she didn't run but stood frozen, ready to take whatever he was about to dish out.

"Caitlin, when did you buy that bar?"

"Two years ago," she answered slowly, quietly.

"When Stash turned twenty-one?"

"Around then, yeah."

"Close to the time he was laid off?"

"He lost his job the week after his twenty-first birthday."

"Under Pennsylvania law you can't own a bar, can you?"

She shook her head, fighting the urge to defend herself.

"Because you have a job, you can't own a bar. So you put the bar in Stash's name, which means he can't work anywhere else—like in the mill. If they ever call him back, he can't go." He stopped talking and studied her, and from the look on his face Caitlin could tell he'd gone past hypothesis and had reached conclusions. "Pretty handy way to keep your brother in college, isn't it?"

For a second Caitlin just stared at Michael. Then she said, "I do what I have to do," as she spun to face the door and darted out.

Four

Even as his car was inching its way across Tillman Bridge in rush-hour traffic, Michael asked himself why.

He knew the obvious reason. He had to apologize. Caitlin hadn't put the bar in Stash's name. She had put it in her mother's name. So, not only was his assumption dead wrong, but he'd really overstepped his boundaries when he'd accused her of manipulating her brother. So he owed her an apology.

But did he really have to cross the river? Couldn't he just do this by phone?

His thoughts went round and round until the four-lane turned into a two-lane and he was forging a path through the fresh snow on the quiet streets of Franklin, the borough that surrounded the mill. Fat white flakes danced in the glow of streetlights, but otherwise everything was still. No sound came from behind the closed doors of big-porched houses with short front yards and no fences. No one had marred the perfection of the white blanket on the sidewalk. Lights were lit, smoke billowed from chimneys and snow fell. Steadily, heavily, round flakes poured to the ground like rain, but more peaceful, more beautiful than rain could ever hope to be.

Michael stepped from his Mercedes and sighed heavily. Why was he doing this? He wasn't the type to be obsessed with a woman. And he didn't want her to think too much about this situation and realize he'd pulled strings to discover the bar was really in her *mother*'s name. He wasn't going to provide an explanation because he didn't want to risk the fireworks of her temper. All he wanted to do was apologize. So why hadn't he just called her?

Stomping his snow-covered shoes on the wooden step of Catz, Michael shook his head. "You're a masochist," he told himself, then pushed open the door.

Noise greeted him immediately. Noise, smoke, sweat and warmth. There was something about a little hole-in-the-wall like this that brought out the male animal in the most sophisticated guy, and before he could stop himself Michael was grinning.

"Hey, Michael, what's up?" Stash called, dropping two drafts in front of two grizzled old men who were totally engrossed in this evening's mud wrestling.

Michael dusted the snow from his shoulders, then draped his black coat over the back of an empty chair that was beside an equally empty table. There were four tables parallel to the long thin bar but the only time Michael had seen anyone use them was when the group had been playing cards.

"Not much," he answered Stash, walking the length of the bar and not finding an empty stool. Standing by the poker machine in the back of the room, he let his gaze move down the length of the place, then glanced at Stash. "What's up here?"

"Deer season in another couple of weeks. What'll it be?"

Michael's brow furrowed. "Just a draft." He positioned himself by the bar's gate and leaned on his elbow. "If deer season doesn't start for another couple of weeks, what are they doing here now?"

Stash grinned. "Talking about deer season," he supplied, as if that said it all, and glanced at his watch. "Well, whaddaya know, it's about time for Cait's nightly visit."

"Uh…yeah," Michael stammered. "I guess it is."

Stash gave him a shrewd smile, then swiped the bar once as he waited for Michael's glass to fill from the tap. "Oh, by the way, your editor, Kiki, came by today. She met me after my last class."

Michael slid a dollar on the bar and Stash set a draft in front of him. "So, what did you think?"

Stash shrugged.

"You remember me telling you that there were other ways you could help your friends?"

Without looking up, Stash nodded.

"If you let Kiki's magazine publish a story about how you work your way out of your troubles, you'll be showing other steelworkers that there's life after a layoff. I think," he said seriously, "you'll help a lot of people who aren't quite sure what to do."

Stash blew his breath out on a sigh. "Yeah, I guess."

"I don't know if it means anything, but I'll be writing the article."

"Yeah, Kiki told me. Look, I've got a test tomorrow. I need to study."

When Stash shifted away, Michael didn't try to stop him. At no time did he push for a story like this. Investigating a crime was one thing, but digging into someone's life and exposing his trials and tribulations was quite another. If Stash wasn't willing, Michael had no intention of pushing him into talking. And he wasn't going to let Kiki bully him, either.

Stash opened his book and Michael glanced around. On his right, the two grizzled guys sat staring, stone-eyed and silent, at the women who were mud wrestling on TV. He turned to his left and saw a red-nosed kid who appeared to be deep in thought, looking the way a person did when he didn't wish to be disturbed. Then, a little farther down, past a skinny woman and two men—one of them just meaty and the other huge—he saw the unforgettable tattoo that he remembered was on Bear's forearm.

"Hey, Bear," Michael yelled, back in the groove of small-bar protocol, where anybody could shout anything at anybody as long as their tone of voice was friendly.

"What?" he growled.

"It's me, Michael Flannery, remember?" Michael asked as he grabbed his beer and started down the bar to where Bear was sitting.

"Oh, yeah, Flannery. Rich kid who may or may not want his teeth rearranged."

"I love my teeth exactly the way they are," Michael said, then laughed. "I thought we settled this little misunderstanding at the anniversary party."

"Yeah, but I heard Caitlin ain't too fond of you again."

Michael sighed. "You're right."

Bear slapped his back. "Women. Who can figure 'em out?" he said, and motioned for Michael to take the seat beside him. "I'm buyin'. What're ya havin'?"

"Actually, nothing," Michael said, showing Bear his full glass. "I came to apologize to Caitlin for something that I said and I think I'd like to have all of my wits about me when I do."

"Smart man," Bear said, then chuckled. "Well, take a seat anyway and keep me company. At least I'll have somebody to talk to until Cait gets here. Lord knows, Stash ain't good company these days."

"I heard that, Bear," Stash said, glaring.

"You was supposed to," Bear retorted. He sighed and turned to Michael. "Can't even get him to go hunting this year. Oh, no. Red alert! Look alive, Michael," he said, jutting his jaw in the direction of the window.

"You can see her? In the dark?" Michael asked, squinting.

"Woman casts a mighty long shadow. Even in a streetlight," Bear replied, then called to Stash, "Hey, I said red alert."

"Red alert!" Stash yelped, and bounced from his stool. "Come on, you guys, let's go! You know Caitlin tells Mom everything she sees."

Immediately someone dashed to the television. With a flick of a wrist, the mud wrestlers disappeared and the nightly news replaced them. Money flew across the counter as Stash paid the man with a thousand points on the poker machine. That man scrambled to the neon box, pulled the cord and plugged it in again. When the lights came on only the rules of the game were showing. A newsman was crooning out a story, and Stash was studying. Even Michael sat up straighter in his chair. Bear followed suit, swiveling his stool to face front and folding his massive arms across his chest as he pretended interest in the telecast.

When the door opened, all was quiet. As usual, Caitlin stopped, pulled her hair from her face and scanned the crowd. For a heartbeat her gaze locked with Michael's. Then she marched into the room like Sherman entering Atlanta.

"This is more like it," she announced to everyone in general and no one in particular. She set Stash's plate on the bar and started unzipping her emerald-green corduroy jacket as she walked to the mounted deer heads. Conversation picked up slowly. Someone asked for a beer. Stash got up and poured.

More confident after this chat with Bear, Michael slipped off his seat. Walking on cat feet, he got behind Caitlin.

"I never would have guessed you were a snitch," he whispered in her ear as he took the shoulders of her coat and slid it off. "But it does make more sense that everybody wants to stay on the good side of your mother than thinking they were afraid of you."

The satiny whisper that tickled her ear sent Caitlin's heart rate into overdrive and her mind into total blankness. It was surprise enough to see him sitting with Bear, and it was a complete shock that he'd come over to talk with her, but the warm mist of his breath in her ear nearly made her faint. Dazed, she turned to face him.

"Miss me?" he asked, then brushed a quick kiss across her lips.

Too stunned to speak, Caitlin only blinked up at him.

"Missed you, too," he said, then brushed her lips again.

"Hey! Hey! None of that in here!" one of the grizzled guys yelped. "No swearing. No gambling. No necking," he chortled, and grinned to reveal he had gums but no teeth.

"You did that on purpose!" Caitlin growled, shoving Michael's shoulder. "You aren't content embarrassing one member of my family. You have to embarrass all of us!"

She darted away, but Michael grabbed her arm. "Look, we need to talk."

She jerked free. "No, thanks."

He caught her arm again and took a deep breath before locking his gaze with hers. "I came to apologize."

Totally amazed, Caitlin gaped at him. "You did?"

"Yeah. I know that your mother owns the bar."

Her whole body went rigid. Her eyes grew round and large with fury. "And just exactly how did you come by that piece of information?"

"I . . ." He glanced at Bear and actually considered lying, knowing that once she discovered he'd dug into her private affairs she was going to be livid.

"No one in the bar would have told you," she said, her eyes narrowing into slits. "That's not the kind of information we share with outsiders."

He didn't feel like an outsider and would bet his last quarter Bear didn't consider him an outsider anymore, either. Still, she'd caught him fair and square. "It's a matter of public record. All you have to do is know where to search, and we reporters generally know where to find anything we want to know," he admitted, then glanced down and sighed. "Look, I was way out of line yesterday," he said, staring at his shoe. He grimaced, swallowed, then looked into her eyes again. "And I'm sorry."

She took a deep breath and turned her head to watch Stash studying, then looked at the long line of people at the bar, then back at him.

"I really am sorry," he said sincerely. "Not for checking into the name on your liquor license as much as for accusing you of manipulating your brother."

"I'm sorry, too," Caitlin said if only to get him to stop talking, because this wasn't the kind of thing they discussed openly around the customers. But once the words were out of her mouth, she realized she meant them. He was doing his job and she was beginning to see he poked only when she was evasive. "I guess I should have told you my mother holds the title to the bar, but I...I..." Realizing she was painting herself into a corner, she stopped talking and glanced at the crowd again. She couldn't very well tell him that she'd deliberately led him to the wrong conclusion because she wanted him to stay away from her, particularly since that would have him hot and heavy on the trail of why she wanted him to stay away from her.

After he tossed her coat across the antlers of a bug-eyed deer, Michael pointed at one of the empty tables. "Let me get you a drink. We'll talk."

She could have refused. She knew she *should* have refused. Now that Stash had dived into his dinner and peace had been restored with Michael Flannery, she could just walk out that door, having learned to be polite and honest with this persistent reporter so he'd leave her alone in the future. But when he pulled out her chair she was lost. No one did things like that at work because that was archaic and chauvinistic and an insult to a working woman. And the men in her family, in her neighborhood, held chairs and opened doors only on their first date or on their honeymoon. It was such an unexpected pleasure to be treated with courtly manners that she smiled and took the seat he offered.

Watching her weaken right before his eyes gave Michael a startling revelation. She could be such a barracuda it was easy to forget she was a lady as much as a woman. He glanced around at the noisy crowd, actually wondered how long it had been since anybody thought of her as anything other than a bar buddy, then tapped her nose. "Be right back."

He strode to the bar but bounded back again. "By the way, what do you want?"

"Uh, some wine," she stuttered, feeling young and foolish and incredibly good. Anybody else in this room would have grabbed her a draft. This man actually remembered women weren't men. "Stash knows which kind." Then she blushed, actually blushed, and wished she could crawl under the table for acting like a schoolgirl or an idiot or both, but Michael just tapped her nose again and strode away.

Too embarrassed to watch him, Caitlin sat studying the mounted deer heads and didn't see him take another quick look at the customers, then slide under the bar gate and find the only stemmed glass in the room. She didn't see him grab the wine bottle, the glass and Stash's only remaining dry towel.

"M'lady," he crooned, dish towel over his arm and stemmed glass in his hand. He set a paper napkin on the table in front of her, then gently placed the glass on top of it and filled the bowl with fruity wine.

She blushed again. Stupidly, girlishly.

He smiled again. Stupidly, boyishly. It had been a long time since he'd wanted to court a woman, sweet-talk her, woo her, make her realize how wonderfully feminine she was. But that's exactly what he wanted to do with Caitlin. He wanted to please her, to make her happy....

Suddenly, amid the noise and confusion of a neighborhood bar right before deer season, Michael felt himself in the middle of a miracle. Just being in the same room with her made him feel wonderful, but in the oddest way. It was like coming home after being gone for a long, long time. And he realized his apology had been only an opening line for what he really wanted—another chance to be with her.

He sat on the chair across from her and reached for her hand. "How was your day?" he asked, feeling again that strange sense of anticipation he'd felt right before he kissed her in the gazebo. He wanted to hear anything, everything. And he wanted to tell her everything.

She smiled sheepishly. "Same as usual for this time of the year. Hectic."

"Yeah? Why?"

"Quarter end, year end, tax time."

"Ah, the curse of accountants."

Her nose daintily wrinkled. "Everybody has their curse. Mine's concentrated into one corner of the year with three deadlines looming like the grim reaper."

He brushed her knuckles with his warm lips. "Does this mean I won't be seeing much of you for the next couple of months?"

Caitlin swallowed as little pin prickles of heavenly delight danced up her arm. When he talked like that, he made her feel as if they'd known each other forever, as if they'd shared drinks and dinners and a million movies. But they hadn't. In fact, they were closer to being enemies than friends. They shouldn't even be talking civilly, let alone holding hands. Yet, they were, and it didn't feel wrong. It felt right.

Knowing she had to leave before things got any more confusing, she drew a deep breath. "Look, I have to go home. I wasn't going to stay," she stuttered when his gaze caught hers and held. "I didn't *mean* to stay." But seeing him had confused her to the point that she'd fumbled with her coat, and then he'd slid it off her shoulders, and then he'd pulled out her chair and poured her wine, and now he was holding her hand. And it all felt perfectly natural—too natural, too nice for enemies.

Releasing her hand, Michael rose. The thing that continually bounced back and forth between them was equal parts of fantasy and fire. He understood the fire part. It was chemistry, physical attraction that just wouldn't quit. However, the fantasy part was still giving him trouble. And from the look on Caitlin's face, she didn't understand it, either.

"You didn't finish your wine."

"Really, I have to get home."

"Where's home?" he asked, then smiled when she frowned, as if undecided about whether to trust him with such a personal tidbit.

On a sigh she decided to trust him. "A few blocks up."

"You walked?"

She nodded and turned away to grab her coat.

Michael plucked his from the chair by the door, fully intending to see her home. There were streetlights, but the area was quiet and deserted because no one was venturing out into the heavy snow. She could be mugged, raped, beaten or murdered and no one would see or hear.

"See ya tomorrow night, Stash," she called, waving. Stash barely glanced up from his book. Michael was waiting by the door when she got there.

"Oh, you're leaving too," she spluttered, blushing furiously. Why didn't he just let her alone? Why did he have to act like a knight in shining armor all night? Treating her like a lady, buying her wine and now walking her home. Didn't he realize nothing could come of this? Hadn't she given him enough hints yet? Was he going to make her come right out and say it?

Suddenly inspired, she said, "I'll walk you to your car."

He yanked open the door and held it while she ventured out into the snow. "No. I'll walk you home."

"Don't be silly," she argued good-naturedly, so he wouldn't realize how much this frightened her. "It's snowing so hard you'll freeze."

"I'll take my chances," he announced, bundling her under his arm.

"No, really," she blurted, shivering because this felt so damned good. He was tall and strong and smelled like everything sexy and male. She struggled to remember that she shouldn't like him, she couldn't like him. Even forgetting her own personal considerations, he was still the enemy and she shouldn't even be speaking with him. In fact, he could be walking her home to try to convince her his story was harmless, so she could talk Stash into letting him write it. He might not be interested in her at all.

Despite all logic, her heart sank. "I'll be fine."

He snorted once. "What if you get mugged?" He swept his free arm through the wall of snow. "No one would even hear you if you—"

Beneath his arm, her shoulders shook, but the giggly laugh she issued stopped his words.

"Mugged? Here?" This time she swept her arm through the snow. "Look around you. These are houses. Nice, neat, respectable houses, inhabited by nice, neat, respectable people."

She tried to slip away, but he tightened his hold on her shoulders. "Sometimes muggers are immigrants."

"Immigrants?" she repeated, puzzled.

"People from other neighborhoods who can't be identified."

"Oh," she said, then laughed again, totally pleased to her feminine toes that he actually cared about *her*, not about a chance to charm her into helping him convince her brother to let him write his story. "What a suspicious mind you have."

He thought about that. Snow wet his hair and chilled his nose. "Not suspicious. Just cautious."

The sincerity, the caring in his voice, stopped her heart. He was amazing. He was the kind of guy you dreamed about but never met. One of those cowboys who could rough it up in the saloon with the best of them but didn't want to. The kind who saved the ranch and made friends with the Indians. The kind she was positive existed only in movies.

The warmth of his arm held her prisoner; his scent enveloped her. But he wasn't pushing for anything other than her company. For the first time in years she felt safe, content, wanted. Around them snow fell. Their breath misted. The silence had an intimate feeling, a kind of peaceful solace that soothed the soul and made one happy for no reason at all. She kicked at the snow with her boot and decided it was time to resurrect their argument before one of them or both of them got any silly ideas. "So, did Kiki call Stash?"

"Yeah."

"What's the verdict?"

"I think Stash's undecided."

The tone of his voice was so casual that Caitlin's brows rose. It sounded as if he could lose this story and wouldn't care, she realized incredulously. She sneaked a quick peek at his face but couldn't make out details in the darkness. Frustrated, she looked away.

Had she blown this out of proportion? she wondered. Was she making a big deal out of nothing? No. Stash couldn't handle the pressure of being the topic of a Sunday review. Still, she had been a little pushy, a little bossy, a little snippy with Michael, instead of trying to reason with him. And he did seem like a reasonable man.

They passed several more feet in silence. Snow and cold kept them huddled together. "I didn't mean to come off sounding like an old shrew," Caitlin confessed into the silent night. "It's just that Stash...well, he doesn't know what he wants. I mean, he knows what he wants but he gets these macho ideas into his head and my dad confuses him and he starts talking like an idiot. He doesn't really want to go back to the mill. He just misses the camaraderie. The beer-drinking, story-swapping good old days when he was one of the crowd. He just wants to belong again."

Michael glanced back at the neon Catz sign. The door opened and Bear stepped into the cold, jerking his coat collar around his ears. He was younger than the guys without teeth and older than the guys who hung around the poker machine, the ones who drank beer from bottles and talked nonstop about their trucks—and so desperate for company he'd befriended a stranger. "Is that so bad?"

Five

―――――

They passed another block in intimate silence. Melting snow sparkled in Caitlin's hair. Fat flakes twinkled in the amber glow of the streetlights. Before morning they'd have six inches, maybe more, but at the moment the snow didn't concern her. Michael's question was so heartfelt, so sincere, it touched her in the oddest way, made her think of herself instead of her brother. Suddenly her own life, her own loneliness, weighed her down.

"In some ways I think I understand," Caitlin whispered.

Confused, Michael turned to face her. "You do?"

She sighed heavily and her breath curled around them. "Yeah."

"Tell me," he coaxed, brushing snow from her hair. His black glove looked big and bulky, totally wrong yet totally right against the satin femininity of her snow-dusted locks. Michael considered it the person-ification of the ironic fit of male and female.

She shrugged. "It's not so hard to understand, really," she muttered, kicking the snow with her boot again. She stopped then and was quiet for such a long time that Michael didn't think she planned on elabor-ating, but suddenly she made a circle with another quick sweep of her hand. "I still live here," she ex-plained. "I go to church here, support the volunteer fire company, get my groceries from Mr. Talbott's store." She paused, thinking, and Michael rubbed his hand down the thick sleeve of her corduroy coat, as if trying to warm her. Actually, he felt more as if he was comforting her, coaxing her into trusting him.

She sighed again. "But it's not the same. I'm really not one of them anymore. I make more money, have a more sophisticated occupation." She lifted her face to the heavens but got snow in her eye and shook her head. "I don't talk the same language anymore, and I really can't empathize with their troubles." She stopped at the bottom of a long, narrow stairway that was enclosed by rickety boards. Michael stopped, too. "I think they're wasting their time by staying here. They're fighting to keep what they have. I think they should move away, improve their lives. They don't want to."

Hearing the hopelessness in her voice, Michael stopped walking and brushed snowflakes from her cheek. Again his big black glove looked oversized and clumsy against her small feminine features. Her dainty face with jeweled eyes and pouty mouth gave her a femininity that somehow made him feel just as big, just as male, just as basic, as Bear. He slid his hands to her shoulders, marveling at how small she was compared to him.

"Their families are here," he said softly, his hand slipping up and down her arms again, comforting, warming. Neither knew which; neither cared. "It's why you stay, too."

She locked her emerald eyes with his brown ones and smiled. "I know."

He felt her smile the whole way to his toes. It warmed him, aroused him, but most of all pleased him. Awed by what was happening between them, Michael stared at her. It seemed that every word, every gesture, formed a bond or broke a barrier. In a scant three days he felt closer to her than he'd ever felt to another human being.

A gust of wind seared his cheek and he put his arm around her shoulders again. "Come on. Let's get you home before you freeze."

He began to walk ahead, but she stopped him. "I am home."

Michael looked at the block building, which was obviously somebody's three-car garage, then glanced up at the aluminum-sided apartment above it. "Oh."

She laughed with delight. "Snob," she said, then laughed again. "Really, it's very nice inside."

"I'm afraid I'll have to see it to believe it."

Her laughter faded, only to be followed by a pregnant silence that stretched awkwardly between them. "Another time."

He should have been pleased that she was admitting there would be another time. Instead, frustration hummed through his blood. He wanted to see her apartment now. He wanted to talk some more. He wanted to kiss her until her taste was branded on his tongue, and then he wanted to make love. And that was the need he couldn't seem to master. He'd never been more aware of the fact that he was a man and his companion was a woman. Small and silent, Caitlin made him feel like an oversized gorilla with a libido just as big and a clumsiness he couldn't control.

"There's snow on your steps," he mumbled inanely, wishing he could be poetic and romantic. But he supposed worrying about her was better than sweet-talking her because sweet-talk and flirting would probably be the end of him. If she as much as smiled too sweetly, he'd be making the kinds of passes decent men didn't make toward decent ladies on what could be construed as their first date. "You could slip and fall."

"The snow's just on the first two steps," she assured him, and moved toward them. "The rest are under the roof."

He might not want to appear overeager, but he wasn't going to be so easily turned away, either. He at least wanted a good-night kiss. His whole life seemed to be hanging in the balance somehow, and though he couldn't figure out why, he knew that if he didn't do something now he'd never get the chance again. Not tomorrow. Not next week. Not ten minutes from now. Unless he kissed her now, he never would.

He grabbed her arm and spun her around, but when he looked at her, genuine concern for her welfare sneaked up on him again. Against the backdrop of the dark building, she looked small and defenseless.

"Somebody could hide in that stairway and wait for you at the top." Nervous, he ran his gloved hand along the back of his neck. Any other time, with any other woman, he'd grab her, kiss her and run for his car. With this one he kept getting conflicting impulses. Like honestly worrying about her when he was supposed to be charming her into a kiss. It was a strange, confusing tug-of-war with rules he didn't understand and no trick up his sleeve to give him the advantage.

She laid a hand on his arm. "No one ever does."

Kicking the snow, he smiled sheepishly. "There's always a first time."

It took a minute for Caitlin to catch on, but when she did, she was flattered to the point of speechlessness. Not because he wanted to kiss her but because he was willing to suffer the agony of her stupidity until she realized what he wanted. He looked big and awkward and acted like a sixteen-year-old angling for his first kiss, and that was cute...sweet...very romantic. His concern—the worry over her steps and the empathy she felt from him as they talked of her life—warmed her even in a snowstorm. She couldn't remember the last time she'd been able to speak so honestly, to let her guard down, to admit her life was less than perfect. She liked him, trusted him, and she wanted to kiss him again, too. "I guess you could always check. You know, go up first and make sure no one's there."

He grinned stupidly. Suddenly, it was a game. He knew it; she knew it. It was a mating dance that pointed out roles, made him feel like a man and her feel like a woman. She knew no one waited for her. She knew she could take care of herself. But he had an overpowering need to take care of her and she was willing to indulge him, even though they were really on their way to a kiss. It was foolish and fanciful and fantastic. He grabbed her hand and led the way.

"Don't you have a light or something?" he grumbled, groping for the banister.

"No. It was awkward at first, but after six years I can find my way blindfolded."

"You might as well be blindfolded," he muttered in disgust, thinking she could slip and fall, kill herself, if someone as much as threw a candy wrapper on one of her steps.

"Yeah, well, Mr. Hanwell didn't plan to put an apartment here. Just by looking at these steps you can see that."

"I'll talk to him," Michael decided, pulling her behind him. He reached the top of the steps, the small enclosed landing, and brought her in front of him. "It can't cost too much to string a light out here."

"You're acting silly," Caitlin giggled, then sobered and wrapped her fingers around his lapels. "We're both acting silly. I don't need a light for these steps—" she met his eyes "—and I really didn't need for you to check for muggers."

"No. You didn't." He couldn't stop looking at her. Her attention was equally focused on him. Sexual awareness and the reason for his climbing the steps thumped between them. But he wanted to do more than climb her steps and kiss her good-night. He could say it. She could refute it. But admitting it, arguing about it, wouldn't change it or stop it. Just by the way she was looking at him, he knew she felt the same way he did, but he never took the look in a woman's eyes as agreement.

"No, you didn't," he said again, then lowered his head and captured her gasp with his mouth.

Frozen nose bumped frozen nose, but the warmth of his lips was everything Caitlin wanted. This was the perfect end to a perfect night. Not something she could talk about or define, just something she wanted.

He lifted his head, and confused by his unexpected withdrawal, Caitlin blinked. Eyes open, he brushed his mouth over hers once, then twice. Trapped in the spell his eyes wove, Caitlin could only stare back as warm tingles rippled the whole way to her toes.

He pulled away again and Caitlin continued to stare at him. What was he doing? Why wasn't he kissing her? Why did he keep looking at her as if she knew all the answers to every question he had? Nervous, she wet her lips. He followed the movement of her tongue with his eyes, then captured her gaze. Again? he seemed to be asking. Can I kiss you again?

Caught off guard by the question in his eyes, Caitlin swallowed. He seemed so serious. Her fingers flexed convulsively on his lapels, then flattened against his chest. She stared at them, stared at his heavy wool coat. She slid her hands from his chest to his shoulders. Her eyes followed them, seeing his size more than his coat. White-gloved hands slipped to his neck, to his nape. Why did her hands look so small on him? Why did her plain white gloves look so feminine? Why did she feel this strange ache that was more emotional than physical? It was an odd sensation, an earthy and basic instinct, but it seemed to mate soul to soul, not body to body. She watched her hands move down his arms, then go back to his neck. Her hands were so small. His shoulders were so big.

When she met Michael's eyes again, he was waiting like an expectant father. Experimentally, she stroked her white wool against the black stubble on his cheeks. Something deep and wonderful was happening between them. She felt like a virgin experimenting with her first touch, discovering her first man. Yet, he didn't push. He waited. Suddenly, instinctively, she knew he felt this way, too. In curious wonder, she watched her white glove slide over his cheek. They were the same, two peas in a pod of confusion outside her front door, but they were different. Her tiny fingers rippled over his stubbled cheek again...so different.

She lifted her green eyes to meet his deep brown ones. She smiled. He smiled. Warmth arced between them as their breaths mixed and mingled. She rolled up onto her tiptoes. He leaned toward her. Warm mouths met, brushed, then clung in sweet fulfillment. He tightened his arms around her, nearly raising her off the rickety porch. Happily spiraling out of control, Caitlin went with the magic.

Wet and wanting, his mouth slanted over hers, awakening a hundred sensations she'd long since forgotten. Beside him, against him, curled into his warmth, she felt like a woman, not an accountant, not a sister, not a bar owner; just a woman. Her head spun with it. Her knees went weak with it. The heady combination of his mouth and his scent were driving her over the edge of her sanity. At this moment, all she wanted, needed, was centered on the strong arms holding her, the wet mouth coaxing her, the sight and size and feel of this man.

He pulled away again, capturing her cheeks with big gloved hands. "Caitlin," he breathed, staring at her with the same kind of wonder that thumped through her body. "This is crazy. I feel like a kid."

And then he was kissing her again. His mouth pressed down on hers until she was struggling for air. Even so, she wrapped her arms more tightly around his neck as he moved his hands restlessly down her back. When they reached her hips, he dug his fingers into her soft derriere and then groaned and pushed her more snugly against him. His kiss became greedy, insistent, as he rocked her hips against his with a gentle motion that was somehow out of sync with the havoc it created inside her body.

Labored breathing was the only sound. The bite of the cold didn't penetrate the heat that enveloped them. There was only need, blinding need, that took away reason and logic and replaced it with primitive instinct.

Kissing her desperately, he struggled with the zipper of her jacket. Just as greedy for the feel of him, she began to unbutton his coat. When her zipper was down and his buttons undone, he crushed her to him again, rubbing his wall of chest against her soft breasts. Heat and need, desire and emotion, collided, then exploded. Frantically, he dipped his fingers under the neckline of her sweater.

Steeped in the magic, Caitlin whispered, "Buttons," then drew his mouth back to hers. For a second he seemed too confused to respond. Then realization dawned and his mouth clamped down on hers even as his fingers fumbled with the tiny pearl buttons that ran the length of her sweater. He released enough only to expose her breasts to his hungry fingers, then cursed roundly under his breath as he stepped away from her.

Coming out of a haze, Caitlin blinked her eyes open to see Michael whip off his gloves and shove them into his coat pockets. She hadn't so much as drawn a second breath before he was kissing her again, probing his cold fingers against the warmth of her breasts.

Suddenly, it was hysterically funny. Inside she was a volcano of need; so was he. Yet her nose was frozen. His fingers were icy cold. But the giggle that bubbled in her throat died a quick death when he rolled a pebbly nipple between his fingers.

"This is insanity," he muttered against her mouth. "I want to touch you, taste you. I want you to shiver with need, not because you're freezing to death."

Still, he didn't give her a chance to answer. His lips closed over hers and his hand stroked to her back, where he undid the clasp of her bra. His fingers warmed even as the skin that warmed them became icy cold from their touch. But when both of his hands closed over her breasts, she shivered with need, not from the temperature. A low, gurgly moan came from her throat as she arched into his hands. White-hot need spiraled through her, making her crazy. They both knew they had to get out of the cold, but neither one seemed to be able to stop long enough to open the door.

The thought was a surprisingly sobering one. What she was doing was making love to a man she hardly knew . . . on her front porch . . . in subzero weather.

Breathing heavily, Caitlin pulled away. He groaned and dropped his forehead to hers. For a long time there was nothing but the sound of their breathing, the thumping of their hearts. A sudden gust of wind shook the rattly frame around them, bringing Michael quickly to his senses.

He drew her coat around her naked breasts. "You're going to freeze."

Pleased that they seemed to be sliding out of this easily, she drew his lapels together, too. "Yeah."

He brushed a soft kiss across her forehead. Too much, too soon, he thought with a heavy sigh. He was pushing too hard and too fast and he knew it, but he'd never met a woman like this, never wanted a woman like this. His instincts were convinced that this was the right time, the right woman. Even though he wanted to ravage, he knew he couldn't, shouldn't.

Despite all that, he pulled her against him again. She burrowed into his warmth. For another minute, they simply breathed. The scent of her drove him crazy. The size of him knocked her for a loop. Gently he petted her back, memorizing every vertebra. With a sigh, she tunneled herself more deeply into his topcoat. He cupped her behind. She slid her hands up his chest, over his vest, across his tie, around the starched collar of his shirt. Her head lifted. His head bent. Eyes open, they watched each other until their lips met again. And then there was nothing but heat and need.

"Caitlin," he said, pulling away from her. "Invite me inside for coffee."

She rested her forehead on his chin. "I can't."

"Please."

Six

She took a deep breath and closed her eyes, well aware that he wasn't really asking for a cup of coffee. He rubbed her shoulders, then let his hands smooth her back, and it felt so good, so heavenly good, to be touched again. She took another breath.

"I only have instant," she whispered.

"I'm not picky."

She looked into his eyes and saw the warmth and passion there. Somewhere inside her soul something snapped. An overpowering, overwhelming instinct sprang to life and she knew she wouldn't say no. Couldn't say no. "Okay."

She turned then because she didn't want him to say anything. With shaking fingers she reached into her pocket for her keys. He took them from her hand, easily unlocking the door.

"This *is* nice," he said after he'd flicked on the living room light.

"It's not fancy," she said, taking off her jacket and hanging it in the closet, while he did the same. "But it's home," she added, and turned to go into the kitchen.

He caught her arm and spun her around, then led her to the couch. She didn't argue or protest. "I don't really want any coffee," he said before he kissed her.

She savored the feeling, the taste, the emotion of his kiss. Opening her mouth. Rubbing her hands up and down his back. Pressing herself against him, steeped in the sensation of having a male body against hers.

He groaned and folded his arms around her, running hot nibbling kisses along her lips, across her cheeks, and back to her lips again. The powerless sensation of the pull of instinct and passion swept through her, telling her one more time that there was no turning back. No compromise. Not this time. Not with this man.

"Michael, if we go to my bedroom, will you promise not to notice the dust?"

"Caitlin, if we go to your bedroom, I probably won't even notice the color of your curtains."

"Okay," she said, taking his hand as she stretched to brush her lips across his, softly, sweetly.

Despite the infinitely gentle touch of her mouth, it evoked vivid sensations and images for Michael. Every wicked fantasy, every pagan dream he'd had since the night he met her, flashed quick as lightning through his mind. Then he looked into Caitlin's eyes, saw she wasn't quite as confident as she'd put on, and all that went out of his head.

He feathered his lips across her cheeks, down her throat. "Tell me what you want," he whispered hopefully.

It took a minute and she had to sigh first, but finally she said, "Everything."

Which told him nothing.

He brushed her eyelids closed with his lips and considered his options. Her soft floral scent teased his nostrils. Her velvet skin tempted his hand. Her lips skimmed his neck. He swallowed.

There was a purely physical everything to be considered here, and then there was that very special communion people achieved when the night was right and the person was right and the passion was beyond control. He was drowning in sensations but it was because of emotions, and he knew that if his passions would ever reach their limits or go beyond, it would be tonight. For him this would be a once-in-a-lifetime experience. For her...

Her lips gently skimmed his neck again, and Michael closed his eyes. The night was right; the woman was right. There'd never be another opportunity like this again. He knew it as surely as he knew their meeting had been no accident. They had been destined to meet, they had been destined to kiss and now they were destined to inspire passion the likes of which neither one of them would know again. The attraction of opposites he'd remember for the rest of his life.

He slid an arm under her knees and kissed her until her arms came around his neck. "Cait?"

"Hmm?"

"How long did you say your parents have been married?"

Drawing away, she blinked up at him. "Thirty-five years. Why?"

"Remember that," he said, then kissed her again. His mouth moved over hers with unrelenting thoroughness, confusing her, arousing her. When her hands drifted from his neck and stroked his back, he started to rise from the couch. Her arms floated to his neck again. Still, their lips never parted. He carried her toward her bedroom, all the while teasing her, caressing her mouth, driving her into delirious abandon. With only one eye open, he kicked open the door, then slid her to her feet.

Still clinging lip to lip, he slipped his hands under her sweater and petted her back and her ribs until she was melting into his hands and her sweater was above her bra. Sweat started beading on his forehead, not from fear but from need. Her skin was like velvet and her breasts just the right size to fill his big hands. Her waist dipped dramatically, then flared out into round, full, perfect hips. Everything he owned tightened and strained toward her. He moaned and smothered her lips with his mouth, all the while counting to forty in an attempt to reclaim his sanity. If he was going to do this, he was going to do it right. Only a fool ruined a once-in-a-lifetime liaison. The passion and spark and fire of ill-fated desire. He'd never find this again. He didn't think she would, either. They weren't just making love. They were making a memory.

Under control again, he positioned his hands under her sweater. When they were angled properly, he broke away. Starry-eyed, Caitlin blinked up at him. Her face disappeared behind her sweater as he pulled it over her head. Then she was gazing at him again, looking flushed and feminine and positively kissable, making him week-kneed with arousal and giddy with desire. He would never, could never, survive this kind of passion a second time around. He was used to something a little tamer, a little more predictable. This was too close, too open, too intimate, for people who hardly knew each other. And yet, if baring her body meant baring his soul, in his eyes, in his raw need, then that was the price he'd pay. This once. This perfect once.

Not giving her the chance to think or protest, he unhooked her jeans, then slid them down her hips. He sank to his knees to drag them off and when his gaze collided with lacy underwear, he swallowed hard, feeling that wonderful tingling tug of need that hit him fast and hard. He felt enslaved by it, and he couldn't stop his tongue from following her jeans as they rode down her legs to her feet.

Caitlin fell to the bed. Vaguely she glimpsed the familiar shiny black lacquer and Oriental designs of her bedroom but couldn't focus on anything but what Michael was doing to her. She didn't know much about seduction, only that she was in the hands of an expert, but the scratch of his tongue on her ankle was so arousing she nearly fainted. Never did she imagine that being undressed could be so sensual, so ritualistic, so much a part of a sexual act, but when he kissed the arch of her foot, Caitlin dissolved to her back, knowing she'd missed a lot in her twenty-eight years. He performed the same wicked miracle on her other foot, but this time he kissed each toe before his hands slipped up her bent legs. The heat of his fingers branded every inch of her legs the whole way to her underwear.

By the time he moved away from her, Caitlin was breathing so hard she knew she'd faint from either arousal or hyperventilation. There wasn't an inch of her he'd left untouched, yet she knew there was more. Wonderful delights saved for the dark of a cold winter night. When the wind howled and snow fell and others went about their business as usual, two people found passion in its most abandoned state and clung to it.

She was almost under control again when he tugged on her fingers. "Come here," he whispered, sitting on the bed. The pull of his hands was enough to help her up, and once she was sitting again, he coaxed her arms to his neck. This time she didn't feel his collar because he'd removed his shirt. Mesmerized, aroused, she stared at his hair-covered chest, then watched her hand as it played over muscle and sinew. She lifted her gaze to his again, and the way he was staring at her made her swallow.

Of their volition their faces moved closer, but when their lips met, they kept their eyes open. There was something so earthy, so basic, about the way he looked at her that Caitlin couldn't get enough. He skimmed his hands along her ribs.

Caitlin whimpered and closed her eyes and in the next second his thumbs were rubbing pebble-hard nipples.

"Oh, Cait," Michael growled, nibbling kisses on her flushed face. "You're making me crazy."

"You're making me pretty crazy, too," she gasped, shocked that her voice sounded so pained. What she felt, what he did to her, was exquisite torture. His hands started moving again, sliding under her bra to whisk it away. It fell to the floor.

"You've got to move up some. Your feet are dangling over the bed."

As if in a haze, she let him move her, shift her, until she was in the center of the bed. Then his mouth closed over hers as his arms encircled her, and she tumbled backward to the bed and outward to blissful insanity. Every inch of her tingled and there was a deafening roar in her ears. There were things she should be saying, doing—she was coherent enough to realize that—but she was so dazed with what he did to her that she couldn't remember what.

His hands played over her skin, robbing her of her last shreds of sanity, as he whispered promises against her lips. Promises of pleasure and passion that she couldn't refute. Promises of happiness and contentment that she didn't quite understand. And then the wind shook the glass in her window and her lacy chastity began crawling down her leg. The glass trembled. Her body trembled. Time and reality spiraled away as his fingers walked up her leg, danced along her thighs, then wove into her most private, most intimate sanctuary.

She would have cried out at the wonder of it all, but suddenly he was kissing her again. The wind was howling now, sounding like the cry of her soul as it was being set free. His fingers were insistent, moving, demanding, promising her the moon and the stars. His mouth was coaxing, nibbling, nipping, arousing her to the point where she could only respond. She stroked his heavily muscled arms, then slid her hands to the coarse hair of his chest. And as the storm raged and his fingers learned all her secrets, Caitlin's trembling hands began their own quest.

His flesh was hot and moist beneath her touch. Rich male hair went from his chest to his thighs and further still where her hands couldn't reach. She learned that when she skimmed his thighs, he gasped. She discovered that when she pressed herself against him he'd groan. She found that if she touched him, the part of him that was his alone, he shuddered and begged.

"Don't stop," he gasped. "Don't ever stop. I need you so much I don't know how I ever got along without you."

And then the miracle happened. Both of them opened their eyes and they stared at each other. Realization shone from emerald eyes; joyous relief poured from the ebony pair. "I want you more than I ever thought it was possible to want a woman," he said, brushing his lips across hers, his chest across her breasts, and his maleness against her femininity.

"I know," she said, closing her eyes. "I know." This time it was a whisper.

"Oh, Cait!" Even as he said it, he pressed her to the bed again. He swung one of his rock-hard thighs over her and pinned her on the velvety warmth beneath her back. His eyes met hers and Caitlin watched them change, glitter, glisten, before he bent and brushed his lips across hers.

He kissed her softly first, running his hands over her breasts, down her sides. But the fire that burned between them was too hot to ignore, and the need inside Caitlin was too deep to explain. Restlessly, she explored his back, even as he became greedy for the feel of her. In a twisting tangle of arms and legs, he rolled to his back touching every inch of her while she luxuriated in the pleasure of discovering him. But when he tumbled her to her back again, their positions had shifted enough that the most natural, most amazing miracle occurred. As his weight settled atop her, she arched and took him into her waiting warmth. Eyes open, they watched each other. He knew her pleasure. She saw his joy. For a minute they simply soaked it all in. The emotion, the sensation—it was in their eyes, in their hearts. Then she lifted her mouth for his kiss and he took it.

Sheathed in warmth and pleasure so intense it bordered on pain, Michael savored her mouth, the taste of her tongue, the feeling of her legs wrapped around him. Filled with him, steeped in him, Caitlin rocked her hips against him until his fingers dug into her derriere.

"Take it easy on me, honey. I'm only human," he said against her mouth.

"Please, Michael," she whimpered, wiggling against him. "It's been so long."

Nothing she could have said would have pleased him more. That she could need him, want him, was arousing enough; but that it had been a long time sent him spiraling into madness. It meant that she felt it, this once-in-a-lifetime something that pushed you over the edge of sanity and sent you spiraling into sensations and need. And though that wasn't exactly a declaration of love, Michael didn't care. What he wanted, needed, was for her to be enslaved by the madness, too.

He clamped his mouth on hers and kissed her so hard she shivered around him. Everything she wanted was here and now. The earthy sound of the storm. The feeling of his big body moving with her, against her. The intimacy she thought she'd never know again.

"Michael," she whispered, fluttering her fingers down his sweat-slicked back. "I think I'm going to cry."

"Oh, don't cry, sweetheart," he groaned. "It's all right."

"It's more than all right," she said, loving him for misunderstanding. "It's perfect. You're perfect." And then she was spiraling out of control, shivering and clinging. This wonderful, intense passion was too glorious, too right, to be an accident. He took her so easily, so naturally, that her body ached. He loved her so easily, so naturally, that her heart ached. Never before had she felt this instant companionship, camaraderie, attraction, all blended together with a passion the likes of which she never dared dream existed. If she were forced to put a tag on her feelings, it would be impossible. No mere word was deep enough, profound enough, to express the way he touched her soul. He'd taken a place in her life so quickly that it almost seemed to have been reserved for him. She knew there had never been, would never be, another man who could accomplish that, but even as he fulfilled every promise of passion, as her body tensed, then skyrocketed, as she clung to him, whispering his name while passion overwhelmed her, shadowy reminders of the consequences haunted her.

The rattle of the wind against her window brought Michael back to earth. He wasn't exactly sure what was happening between them, but anything this great couldn't be bad. He rolled to his back, dragging her with him so she was nestled against his side.

He kissed her forehead, then closed his eyes and let himself sink back into the oasis of fulfillment and contentment.

She hesitated, afraid of the consequences of getting too close, sharing too much. As it was she'd already gone too far. She pulled away from him and turned to glance at the clock. "My God! It's only seven-thirty. You must have driven to Catz without even stopping for dinner."

He grabbed her arm and pulled her over to him again. "I did," he said, shifting to his elbows until he was looking down at her. Slowly, silently, he studied every inch of her. "Has anyone ever told you you are absolutely beautiful?"

"No one," she said, inching away from him.

He caught her wrist and slid her over to him again. "Don't."

"Don't what?" he asked, sounding mesmerized, still staring, still steeped in the afterglow of spent passion. A luxury she couldn't afford.

"Don't look at me like that!" she said, and frantically groped for the black velvet bedspread. She tried to flip the heavy blanket over her, but it slapped his face, then settled on his shoulder.

"It's a little late for modesty," he said in a whisper, then flipped it away again. "Anyway, I want to look at you. I love to look at you."

Her face got so red with embarrassment her cheeks even felt hot. "You're making me feel like a harlot."

"Why? Because I like the way you look?" he asked her, even as his fingers traced a thin line that went from her stomach to her breast. When he lifted his eyes, they were dancing with pleasure. "The way you feel?"

She felt the dizzying pull again, the uncontrollable desire to lift her head the slightest bit so he'd bend and kiss her. "No," she mumbled, swallowing. "Look, could we pull the cover up or something?"

"Why?" he asked, sounding totally confused. "You're perfect, Cait. It's one of the reasons you drive me crazy."

"Please?" she asked, grabbing the cover again.

He gave her a puzzled frown, but an expression of realization followed on its heels. "Oh, you're shy," he said, then kissed her lips. "Okay, we'll go for the covers."

It wasn't easy and it wasn't neat, but the second Michael rolled away from her, Caitlin started moving. By the time he was sliding beneath the decadent black spread, Caitlin had been there for a minute and a half. In the silence that followed she pressed her lips together as tears pooled in her eyes. There was a part of her that was irresistibly drawn to him, that wanted to roll across the three feet that separated them and just hold him.

Just hold him.

After what she'd already done, holding him didn't seem like that much of a crime. And it wasn't, until you got your perspective and realized that the intimacy, the emotion, the real sharing, came now.

She took a deep breath. "Why don't I make you an omelet?"

"Why don't we stay right here for a while?"

She swallowed, feeling those damned tears again and fighting herself more than him. "I'm not used to this, Michael," she whispered, desperately working to keep the quiver from her voice. "I'm not comfortable."

He was silent for a few seconds. Then he said, "Okay." He sat up and reached down to gather his clothes. "I'll dress in the bathroom."

"Thanks," she whispered as a lone tear ran down her cheek.

"But I want the omelet," he said, turning to face her.

She nodded, grateful that they hadn't turned on the light, because she was crying so hard tears were rolling to her pillow and it was difficult to keep the sound muffled.

"And we're going to talk about this."

She nodded again, knowing she'd think of some logical story, some good reason, to get him out of her life, long before he was finished eating his omelet.

Seven

When Michael came to the kitchen Caitlin was whipping eggs, even though she'd taken the time to dress completely. Jeans. Sweater. Bra. Underwear. Socks. Shoes. Everything. She'd even combed her hair. This was going to be difficult enough as it was; she didn't want to be wearing a robe, feeling intimate, expressing intimacy. To pull this off, she was going to have to appear either cold or crazy. Neither idea comforted her, but at least fully dressed she could do one or the other with dignity.

Caitlin cast a sideways glance in Michael's direction, noting that he looked as good as he had when she first saw him in Catz. He had combed his hair and buttoned his shirt, which was neatly tucked into his dress pants. His watch was in place. Even his shoes were tied. He'd dressed as completely as she had—not because he had any hang-ups or inhibitions, but because she'd given him the impression she was riddled with them. And, she realized suddenly, he'd allowed her plenty of time to get dressed and run out of the bedroom.

Maybe the old shy routine didn't seem as stupid and inane as she'd thought. Maybe she should just keep going with that—especially since anything was better than pretending you were crazy.

"Your omelet smells wonderful, " he said as he pulled a chair away from her table.

"I hope you like green peppers," she said, turning to face him, but he looked so good, so perfectly handsome and male and so natural sitting at her table, that she had to face the stove again.

"I love green peppers," he replied enthusiastically.

"Good," she said, filling an awkward silence that began to slide into the room. She'd never been caught in this quandary before, totally and completely smitten, not just with a man but with the idea of being in love . . . of having a mate, a companion.

"You know, Caitlin," Michael began, and Caitlin faced him again. "I generally don't sleep with a woman until I've known her for a long time."

The silence fell again just as the browning vegetables and butter began to sputter. Gratefully, Caitlin pivoted to complete her cooking.

"In the bathroom," he continued, quietly, slowly, and in her mind's eye Caitlin could almost picture him playing with the silverware to cover his awkwardness at confronting this situation, "I realized that I probably seem like a real—I don't know, creep, womanizer, something, to you because I really did come on a little strong out there on your porch and I did sort of force you to let me walk you home and I virtually begged you for a good-night kiss.... Say something, Cait. I'm drowning here."

She took a deep breath. "Michael, I didn't do anything I didn't want to do. I think we both realize that."

"Then what's wrong?"

"I haven't made love with anyone for a long, long time," she said, still turned away from him. "What I felt for you was so profound, so overwhelming, that I couldn't fight it."

"There's nothing wrong with that."

Under normal circumstances, which happened between two normal people, she wouldn't argue with him. Considering not just herself but him, as well, she had to take issue, albeit nonverbally. "Let's just not discuss it."

"I think we have to discuss it," he said, grabbing her wrist as she set his plate in front of him.

She calmly, easily, twisted her arm from his grasp. "I'll get the coffee."

"Dammit! Cait!" he shouted, springing from his chair and catching her before she reached the counter. He took her shoulders and spun her around. "If we don't talk about this, I get the distinct impression that I'll never see you again."

Looking into his warm brown eyes, seeing a hundred things she'd miss about him, she said, "Actually, that's the plan."

"Why?" he asked incredulously.

She shrugged. "We're different. Ridiculously different," she said casually, and extricated herself from his hold. "Just look at the differences in the way we live. I live above a three-car garage. You live in the penthouse of your own personal apartment building. It just wouldn't work."

He grabbed her shoulders and spun her around again. "That's bull."

She shrugged out of his hold again. "Michael, I've seen things like this happen a million times. One of us will end up giving up their heritage."

"Fine. I've never been too fond of my parents anyway."

In spite of her attempts not to, Caitlin laughed. "I'm calling your mother."

"She'd probably say 'so? Big deal.'"

Caitlin clicked her tongue as she poured him a mug of coffee. To prevent him from grabbing her again, she handed it to him. "Help yourself to sugar and cream," she said, then turned to pour herself a cup of coffee.

"I'm not going to disappear just because you want me to."

"I never asked you to disappear," she said, smiling as she took the seat catty-cornered from him. "I'm simply warning you that I'm not going to go out with you. I'm not going to sleep with you again."

He sighed. "You are ridiculous."

She shrugged. "Perhaps."

"No perhaps about it," he said, and dug into his omelet. "Stubborn, shortsighted—"

"Just like my dad," she said, reminding him that he'd already told her this.

He scowled at her. "I've never, ever, met a woman like you," he said, then took a sip of coffee. "You're not going to like this, but I'm going to get a little graphic here because I think it's warranted. You responded to me, Cait. We were great together.''

"That's a basis for nothing," she said. "What do you want from me, Michael? We've only known each other a few days."

"Precisely," he said, then leaned over and kissed her nose. "Not nearly long enough for you to give me the old heave-ho. If you think I'm giving up, you're crazy. I like you enough that I want the opportunity to explore this relationship. And basically, there's not all that much you can do to stop me."

"There are many, many things I can do. Or should I say, can't do. Like go out. Like to Catz. Michael, if I really wanted to I could lock myself in this apartment for the next six months. I have that much leave accrued at Barnhart Steel because I haven't taken a vacation in the six years I've worked there."

"Fine. I'll serenade you from the street. Oh, and by the way, I have a horrible singing voice. Cats will be joining me. Dogs will be howling. It'll get so bad you'll be begging me to come inside."

She could see it. She could see him, standing in the snow surrounded by baying dogs and crying cats. "You're an idiot."

He leaned across the table again and assaulted her with soft, sweet, nibbling kisses that tasted like warm butter, sweet pepper and smoky bacon. In spite of her better judgment, Caitlin moved forward, sliding her tongue across his warm lips. Tasting him one last time.

"Let's go back to your bedroom," he suggested against her mouth.

"No," she mumbled.

He leaned a little closer. "I could probably get you to change your mind."

"I don't doubt that for a second. But I don't want to change my mind."

He stretched closer again, taking her shoulders in his hands and pulling her to stand. Then he slid his hands down her arms, across her hips and up her back. All the while he sprinkled kisses, warm, sweet, buttery kisses, across her lips.

"You are not fighting fair."

"I'm beginning to see that this is war. And all is fair in love and war. So either way you look at it, I'm within my rights."

"I suppose you are," she said, and let herself be swept away by the magic again. Just one more kiss. One really good, really special kiss. Then she'd back away, back off, and not be seduced into going against her principles.

She rolled onto her tiptoes, meeting his mouth, spreading her hands against the broadness of his back. Slowly, skillfully, he massaged her muscles, and the wind began to howl again. The windows of her apartment shook and her furnace rumbled to life. She tightened her hold on his neck, stretching to get every last second of this final kiss, feeling the heat, rejoicing in the need, the desire, he ignited in her. And she felt herself spiraling again, tumbling into instinct, as the wind cried and the furnace growled and an unknown thump, thump, thump sounded far-off and lonely.

Suddenly, the thumping stopped.

"Caitlin?"

It was almost as though the wind was calling her, maybe scolding her, as it moaned through the trees. She ignored it.

Thump. Thump. Thump.

The kiss grew, deepened. He filtered his fingers through the hair at her nape, slid them along the slim column of her throat, then traced the neckline of her soft sweater. When he reached the smooth pearl buttons, he slipped them, one by one, through their loops, and for every button he freed, he dropped a kiss on her lips.

"Caitlin?"

This time the call of her name in the wind was clearer, louder, and she wondered if she was going crazy, if all the years of deprivation had made her the victim of inner ghosts that would haunt her for the rest of her life.

His fingers lay beneath the soft knit of her sweater, and the skin on which they lay pulsed with the age-old cry for more. The need to touch and be touched sprang up again, but this time she recognized a pattern, a reason. She wasn't responding to instinct or need; she was responding to him. Wanting him. Desiring him. Perhaps even loving him.

He bent his head and touched his lips to hers, smoothing them sleekly from one corner of her mouth to the other before he kissed her fully, sensually, yet with that touch of tender emotion that took away rational thought the same way a light breeze could snuff out a candle.

Hungry hands started opening buttons again. This time her hands, his buttons. Her tiny fingers slid into the forest of rich black hair on his chest and both of them groaned.

Suddenly, there was a knock on her front door.

"Caitlin?" A voice called. A voice that sounded to be just beyond the door.

One of Michael's eyes opened. Both of Caitlin's eyes opened.

"My mother," she whispered, suddenly feeling fifteen. Her fingers flew to her sweater.

Michael jogged to the door and pulled it open. "That you, Mrs. Petrunak?" he asked stupidly as he quickly rebuttoned his shirt. Behind him, Caitlin groaned. "Shh! And get that guilty look off your face!" he commanded in a hissed whisper.

"You're pretty good at this, aren't you?" Caitlin remarked, her fingers fumbling with her slick pearl buttons. "You must have had lots of practice."

"Now is not the time to get jealous, Caitlin. Just try to relax and look like we weren't about to make love."

"We weren't!"

He turned and grinned. "Wanna bet?"

"That you, Michael?" Colleen called up the steps.

"Uh, yeah," he stuttered.

The thumping started again. "Oh, well, hello again," Colleen called.

"Hello to you, too," Michael said, and smiled genuinely at the woman trudging up the steps. When he noticed the big bag in her hands, he scrambled to help her. "Here, let me get that . . ." Reaching for the bag he saw the hem of her flannel gown beneath her long coat and below that, snow-covered pink slippers. "What's this?"

Chin quivering, Colleen looked up at Michael. In another thirty seconds, Caitlin was behind him, shivering, clutching her arms. Colleen swallowed convulsively, but her sobs won out and before they knew it she was wailing like a banshee.

"Oh, Mom!" Caitlin yelped, scampering around Michael. "Mom...what's the matter?"

"Your dad..." She stopped and gulped for air. "That woman...Kiki...came by the house." Heavy sobs convulsed her chest and for a minute Caitlin comforted her.

"What did Kiki do?" Michael asked, thinking he never should have let Kiki be a part of the discovery process. Even though she'd begged, even though he wanted her to learn, he should have refused because of the sensitivity of this particular story.

Colleen batted a hand even as she reached into her coat pocket for a tissue with the other one. "Ah, she didn't do nothing," Colleen muttered. She raised her eyes to look at Michael and sat on the step. Caitlin sat on the step above her mother and rested her hand on Colleen's shoulder. "She came by and explained to me and Dad what she wanted to do for Stash, and Dad got mad and started screaming at her." She looked guiltily at Caitlin. "And I let him," she said, then started to sob again.

Over the bobbing head of the distraught woman, Michael caught Caitlin's eye, but her lips thinned and she looked away. "Then what happened?" she asked softly.

"I...well, I waited until she was gone and then I lit into that old coot! Idiot," she muttered, then blew her nose. "Male chauvinist pig!"

Caitlin would have laughed if her mother hadn't been crying. "Then what happened?" she asked again.

"I...he..." She stopped and thought, clearing her throat. "I said I thought Kiki was right." She glanced at Michael. "This isn't really a story about Stash. It's a story about every one of us. But your dad doesn't like the idea that Stash's whole life will be exposed."

For the first time ever, Caitlin agreed with her father. It struck her as odd, struck her as miraculous. Then her mother started to cry again.

"You mean you think Stash should set himself up as a guinea pig?" Caitlin asked incredulously.

"He won't be a guinea pig," Michael said, stooping beside Mrs. Petrunak. "And the choice is his. You know that, Cait." His eyes held Caitlin's briefly, but long enough to have a heated confrontation. He turned to Colleen. "So then what happened?"

"Me and Dad fought," she said sadly, but suddenly lifted her chin. "And just like you said, Caitlin, I wouldn't let him push me around. I stood up to him like you always said because this is something I believe in."

This was not something Caitlin believed in. Any other controversy, any other argument, she'd have stood behind her mother a hundred percent, but not for this one. "Then what happened?"

"I left him," Colleen announced proudly. "He said, 'If you can't do as I say, woman, there's the door.' And I said, 'Look, you stupid old man, times are changing.' But he pointed at the door again. And I said to myself, Self, it's now or never. You either stand up to him like Caitlin said, or he'll boss you around until you hit the grave." She gave Caitlin a watery smile. "And here I am."

Caitlin looked at Michael again. With his eyes he told her to keep her specific opinions to herself on this because her mother needed her. With one flash of fiery green eyes, she told him the battle might be lost but the war was far from over. For once in her life she agreed with her father, but she had a sobbing mother on her doorstep.

"I did the right thing, didn't I, Caitlin?" Colleen asked suddenly.

"Yes," Caitlin agreed with a sigh. "He sort of kicked you out, so you had no choice."

"He *did* kick me out!" Colleen sputtered indignantly. "He said I had to agree with him or go. I don't agree with him."

"Well, I think I'd better leave," Michael announced as he rose and began walking up the steps to get his coat. The conversation was about to get very personal and he shouldn't hear it. He went inside, looked longingly at the omelet he was leaving, sighed once in the direction of the bedroom and then stepped onto the porch again. Caitlin and her mother were huddled on the step as though Colleen was still a little too distraught to realize she should be freezing.

He stepped around Colleen but stopped by Caitlin, angling his body so Colleen couldn't see him brush Caitlin's cheek. "I'll call you."

She jerked away. "Don't bother, troublemaker," she warned in a whisper. "Now do you see what I mean about our differences?"

"Cait, this has nothing to do with us."

"Maybe you don't care about your family, but my family is all I have. You stay the hell away from us!"

Eight

For the second Sunday in a row, Caitlin found herself marching toward the chrome and glass of Flannery Towers. Rain bombarded her umbrella and her shoes were beginning to squeak, but Caitlin ignored the unpredictable November weather and her undependable shoes as she yanked open the door. This time when the royal doorman approached her, she narrowed her eyes.

"Is he in?"

"Yup. I'll ring you—"

She grabbed his arm before he could reach the phone on the long, thin counter by the door. "Oh, no, you don't," she growled. "I want to surprise him."

"Company policy," he muttered, twisting his wrist out of her hand.

"Hang your company policy. I'll take full responsibility."

He shook his head. "I'll get full responsibility," he informed her, pointing at the gold name tag, which said Phil Jeffreys, pinned to his chest. "Whether you want to take it or not." He lifted the receiver and started punching numbers.

Not in the mood to quibble over stupidity, Caitlin darted behind the thin counter, followed the phone cord and yanked it from the wall.

"What the..." Phil sputtered as Caitlin walked away with the phone, even though he still clung to the receiver.

"Lady, you're going to get me fired!"

Caitlin's chin lifted. "I said I'd take full responsibility. So, if you'd give me that receiver, it'll look like I grabbed the phone before you had a chance to stop me, and you'll be in the clear."

Phil scrubbed a hand over his mouth as he eyed one-inch fingernails. Then he shook his head as he sighed with disgust and tossed the receiver to her. With that he turned away.

Triumphant, Caitlin strode to the elevator. There were six buttons. She pushed the one for the penthouse, and the elevator doors swooshed closed as the little box purred to life. It seemed only two seconds had passed before the bell pinged and the doors swooshed open again. Phone under her arm, Caitlin marched down the hall but stopped suddenly. Hmm, muffins. Homemade blueberry muffins. She raised her nose and sniffed again. Somebody in this building was about to get very lucky.

The sound of a door slamming brought her out of her reverie. She looked right, then left, then realized she hadn't seen any numbered doors in this hall. Her gaze fell to a cherry-wood table, then rose to a painting above it...oh-oh...

"That you, Kiki?"

Oh-oh. First she'd invaded his apartment. Now it appeared she'd be interrupting a rendezvous, too. This is what you get for being so pushy! she yelped in her head. Surprising is one thing, invading another. No wonder he had such a persistent doorman!

"Your mother said you...oh, it's you."

He'd rounded a corner from the back of the long, and—she noticed now—well-decorated hall and stood wiping his hands on a dish towel. His wavy black hair was neatly combed, his clothes were jeans and a T-shirt, but an apron hung from his neck to his legs. The sight of him, just the sight of him, locked her knees and turned her thighs into jelly. Feelings and sensations tumbled through her. Heat and need. Frozen fingers. Wet kisses.

He jutted his black stubbled chin at the phone she was holding. "You expecting a call?"

The mockery in his voice brought her quickly to her senses. "No, I'm not expecting a call," she answered, shoving the phone into his stomach. "This is yours. I grabbed it so the doorman couldn't warn you I was coming up."

"Ah, you wanted to surprise me. Aren't you sweet?"

She would have smacked him for that if she didn't have so many other things she wanted to smack him for. "No, I wanted to make sure you couldn't sneak out when you heard I was coming up."

"How practical," he muttered, setting the phone on the cherry-wood table. "Well, come on, get it over with. Scream at me, punch me." He snapped his fingers. "I know, threaten to sue."

That he could laugh about this, tease about this, only made her all the more furious. "You don't have enough money to compensate for the pain and suffering I've been enduring over the past few days!"

"Because Kiki's got her story?" he asked skeptically. "I don't see how that—"

"Because my mother's in my spare bedroom!" she shrieked, grabbing his apron and jerking him forward. "My mother's a docile little mouse who's never, ever, stood up to my father until you decided to play Good Samaritan and help my brother—even though Stash didn't need help—and so you—"

He peeled her hands from his apron. "Maybe you'd like to blame me for the war in the Persian Gulf, too? How about the Black Plague? It was before my time, but surely there's a way you can stretch the facts until I or one of my ancestors is responsible...."

"Don't you make fun of me," she yelped. "This is serious! My parents—my married-thirty-five-years parents—have separated and it's your fault."

Michael heaved a persecuted sigh. Logic would never work with this woman, not where her family was concerned. The contacts he'd made might report that she was a cool-headed professional. Rumor might have it that she was a sweet little thing who shopped for her elderly neighbor. And gossip, the just plain gossip he'd instigated at Catz, might confirm that she was quiet and shy and about the best first baseman in Franklin's history. But just touch her family and you wouldn't come away with all your fingers. Already he'd had his nipped several times. And God knows his sanity was gone; otherwise, he wouldn't see her point. In a certain sense, her troubles were his fault.

He rubbed his hand along the back of his neck, then began to remove his apron. "All right. Calm down," he soothed, combing his fingers through his hair. "Come into the living room. We'll talk."

"Talk?" she sputtered as he took her arm and started leading her down the hall. "I've had enough of your talk! I want some action."

Everybody else in the world got along with her. Everybody else in the world thought she was quiet, sweet. And everybody said she didn't have a nasty bone in her body. So why was she always yelling at him? He shoved her into the living room. She nearly landed on the chintz couch.

"Exactly what would you like me to do?" he demanded, his patience nearing its limit.

"It's your story..." she started to shout, but felt her voice weakening as she looked around. She'd been expecting a vulgar display of wealth and grandeur. Instead, there was a worn couch and chair and one braided rug. Twin glass lamps on cherry-wood tables were well polished but old-fashioned. So was the spindly-legged coffee table in front of the couch. Only the white brick fireplace and the vertical blinds on a sliding glass door that undoubtedly led to his balcony in any way resembled what she'd been expecting. Confused, she scratched a hand through her hair.

"So?" he asked through a long-suffering sigh. "It might be my story, but Stash agreed."

"Yeah," she muttered, glancing around as she remembered her rain-soaked shoes. Everything around her was probably antique—even the rug—and her shoes were ruined, her jeans damp. To sit down would be sacrilegious.

As she stood looking horribly confused and oddly out of sorts, Michael studied her. She'd run out of steam so quickly he didn't know what to think, say or do. He folded his arms over his chest and waited while Caitlin walked over to the entrance and slid out of her shoes. His brow furrowed. She smiled sheepishly.

"Wet," she explained, shrugging. "I don't want to ruin your furniture or your rug."

"I have this furniture," he said, pointing at the worn couch, "and this rug—" he pointed at the floor "—so people will feel comfortable in my house. Not feel they had to take their shoes off." He stopped, eyeing her quizzically as a blush crawled up her cheeks. This was the woman he'd heard so much about. The sweet, soft-spoken woman everybody adored. The woman he'd courted in a bar. The one he'd walked home in a snowstorm. The one who'd seduced him without even trying. He liked the spitfire, the part of her that stood up for her family with as much brass·as his desk lamp, but it pleased him every bit as much that she could turn around and be so sweet, so considerate. In a roundabout way it proved that she liked him, even though she obviously didn't want to.

"It was my grandmother's," he said with a smile. "I didn't get to visit her often, but when I did I wished

I lived with her. She didn't yell about my shoes, didn't care when Kiki or I jumped on this couch." He thumped it twice. "Once Kiki broke this lamp," he said, pointing at the one beside him. "But Bubba just hugged her until she stopped crying, then picked up the pieces and glued them together again."

No longer angry, Caitlin rubbed her hands along her upper arms. "My grandmother was a lot like that, too." She looked at the furniture with new understanding, then glanced over at him and smiled. "She's been gone for years and years and years, but I still remember her voice... how her house smelled." She drew a deep breath and caught another whiff of muffins. "Speaking of smell..."

"Oh, my gosh! My muffins. Take off your coat, I'll be right back."

While he was gone, Caitlin removed her coat, then slid her fingers across the dust-free surface of an old, scarred table. How did she yell at a man like this? He entered carrying a tray with coffee and piping-hot muffins and Caitlin decided she couldn't. She sank to the couch and stretched out her legs as she sighed. "Sorry about yelling."

"Hey, that's okay," he accepted, squeezing her arm. "Tell me about your pain and suffering."

"Oh, it's awful!" Caitlin moaned. "My mom's so lonely and out of sorts she's driving me crazy! She gets up when I do, cooks breakfast, packs a brown-bag lunch, criticizes my clothes, scrubs my apartment, cooks supper and then badgers me until I sit down and watch TV with her all night."

"I noticed you didn't bring Stash his supper," he said, then waited, the sentence hanging in the air like an accusation.

She knew what he was driving at. She'd threatened to stay away from him and now it looked as though she had. All she'd have to do would be to say that and she could automatically sever their bond. But the truth was she hadn't avoided him. She'd thought about him and pined for him and even cried herself to sleep once. Every time she bit into one of her mother's delicacies she thought of him because he was, after all, the reason her mother was living with her. She couldn't step out of her apartment without remembering his kisses; and when the snow disappeared, she felt a loneliness she couldn't define. But he couldn't know that. Not now. Not ever. All the same, she needed his help and to get it, she'd have to stop insulting him and hope he didn't take that as encouragement. She shook her head. "No."

"Why not?" he asked, handing her a muffin.

She took it, nibbled at it, then set it on a napkin because she was too upset to appreciate it. Not only were her parents separated, but she was dealing with a man who wasn't going to let her hide from him, lie to him or be vague with him. She tried anyway. "It just seemed like a good idea to let Mom do it."

"Why? To give her something to do?"

The noisy breath she took expanded her chest. Admitting this was the tough part. "No. I was hoping Dad would be at Catz." Her gaze drifted over to Michael's. "Because he was as miserable as Mom was." *As miserable as I was.*

Michael shook his head sadly. "He never came in. Not once all week."

"Not once all week?" she repeated, then held her breath. Once or twice she could understand, but all week? "You were at Catz every night this week?"

Taking a long time with his coffee, Michael thought about his answer. "Yeah."

His devotion was every bit as flattering as it was frustrating. No one—and she'd turned away many a suitor—had ever been as persistent as this man. "Why?"

Once again he considered his answer before looking Caitlin right in the eye. "I think I went to Catz every night for the same reason you're here now."

"You wanted to yell at yourself?"

He tweaked her nose. "No, I wanted to yell at you—until Thursday. Then I wanted to kiss you senseless. Then on Friday, I just wanted to talk to you. By Saturday, I'd have settled for just seeing you. But when I woke up this morning with a hangover, I wanted to wring your pretty little neck. That Bear drinks like a fish! Don't ever try to keep up with him."

"You tried to keep up with Bear? Oh, I love it! Don't you know he holds every beer-drinking record in the state?"

"I do now!"

She started to laugh. "Whatever possessed you to do something so stupid?"

Her laughter only made him feel all the more stupid. Bear had been down in the dumps because he wasn't as smart as Stash, and Michael had been feeling equally depressed, and one beer had led to another. By the end of the night, Bear was declaring that he didn't give a damn if he didn't know the meaning of half the words Stash used, while Michael proclaimed that he could live happily without a certain redheaded woman. In a rainstorm, singing old college songs everybody knows, Michael and Bear had felt pretty good. But this morning Michael had awakened as lonely as he had every day all week, and he doubted if Bear felt any smarter.

Depressed again, Michael slumped down on the couch. "Just shut up!"

"Oh, poor baby," Caitlin crooned, getting an odd stirring of happiness because he'd been miserable enough to drink himself silly. She felt herself spiraling into the magic again, into the world where she was allowed to flirt and sweet-talk, where logic didn't matter and dreams still came true. "Did you take some aspirin?"

"Only half a bottle." He pushed her hand away when she went to stroke his temple. "Anyway, what do you care? You threatened me with evil punishment if I didn't let your family alone, and it looks like you got your wish."

"I didn't wish this on you," she said, walking her fingers up his chest. "Come on now, don't be nasty when I'm trying to be nice."

He caught her fingers. What she said made a hell of a lot of sense. He raised two very serious, very dark eyes to catch hers. "Exactly why are you being nice? Any other time you'd be chomping my hand off at the wrist."

"I never bit your hand off at the wrist," she gasped.

He tugged on her fingers until she was almost across him. "Yes, you do. Every chance you get. First you're nice, then you bite. So, if you're here to bite, get it over with and then leave me in peace.''

His accusation made her feel awful, especially when she realized it was true. He probably thought she was a fool. She wished that she could tell him, be honest with him, about why she had to stay away from him, but that generally made things worse. It was better just to argue the obvious, take advantage of the frivolous and keep your secrets in the dark. She drew in a gusty sigh. "All right. So I overreacted a little bit—"

"A little bit?" he echoed in disbelief.

"All right, a lot! But you *have* to understand I was only trying to protect my brother."

"Who's twenty-three."

She tried to get away.

"All right. I get the picture. Stash can take care of himself."

He held her right where she was. "So why are you here? If you're willing to accept the fact that Stash is a grown man who can do what he wants, why are you here?"

Her mouth turned down into a pretty pout. "Because you started this. And my parents—"

"Uh-uh, I don't buy that."

"What do you mean, you don't buy that!" she sputtered. "*You* started this. *You* are the reason behind my parents' split. *You* have to get them back together again."

"Nice try." He infuriated her further by pulling her closer. "But I still don't buy it."

She attempted to struggle out of his arms but succeeded only in getting herself more securely caught. Trying to be stern, she glared at him. "I really don't

care whether or not you believe me," she patiently
enlightened him. "And I see it was a pretty stupid
idea. But I was mad enough and desperate enough to
think..."

"Go on," he prodded when she fell silent.

Both of her hands were caught in one of his and his
other arm was around her shoulders. She felt foolish
and awkward and he felt warm and wonderful. She
drew a deep breath. He smelled like heaven, muffins
and male musk. "And I was foolish enough to think
you'd be able to..."

She stopped again, this time closing her eyes. As the
scent of him trapped her and his warmth enveloped
her, the desire to just melt in his arms swamped her.
How had they come to this so quickly? In eight years
of avoiding men and relationships, she'd never had the
problem of overwhelming physical attraction. Until
now. And that little glitch was causing a dizzying
conflict between what she wanted to do and what she
had to do. Suddenly wrong felt right and right felt
wrong and God only knows what happened to her
ability to think. It seemed all she could do was feel.

"Say it!" he demanded, jerking on her hands.
"Open your eyes and say it!"

"All right! Dammit! I thought you could help!"

He grinned foolishly. "So what you're really saying is that you came to me for help."

"No, I'm saying this is your fault, so you *have* to
help."

"Uh-uh," he whispered, bending to brush his lips
across hers. "You came to me for help, because you
trust me."

When he moved away, she glared at him. "I definitely *don't* trust you."

"Oh, you trust me," he chortled, totally steeped in male pride because he had her this way, pinned physically and emotionally. "Yourself, now that's another story."

"Don't flatter yourself."

"Oh, I rarely have to," he teased, letting his mouth roam over her temple and down her cheek. He watched her eyes close, watched her little grimaces of defeat. Then he released her hands and she sat as still as a mouse, eyes closed, barely breathing. Victory shot through him like a storm. "You're not fighting anymore."

She sighed noisily. "I know."

He removed his arm from her shoulders. "You could run."

She didn't move. "I know."

"In another thirty seconds, I'm going to kiss you," he warned her quietly.

"I figured that out, too." Still she didn't move.

He actually counted to thirty, giving her the fair chance. She still didn't move.

"Caitlin." He said only her name, touched only her hair.

She stretched to meet him. "Michael."

The first kiss was a greeting. Slowly, silently, they said hello. Then he wrapped his arms around her waist and she slid her arms around his neck. In another thirty seconds, they were bound close, lips clinging, bodies straining, molding.

"Caitlin, this is so crazy," he moaned against her mouth. "Why can't you admit that you're as attracted to me as I am to you?"

"Because it's only physical . . ."

"Baloney."

"Because I don't want to be attracted to you."

He thought about that. "Well, that's certainly not a nice thing to hear, but it's honest," he began, then glanced down and saw her looking at him with so much longing in her eyes that it instantly negated everything she'd said.

"Caitlin," he breathed before his lips brushed across hers again. "Why are you doing this to us?"

This time his kiss was a coaxing nibble, a heated touch of his mouth desperately seeking hers. It wasn't a physical meeting of two mouths; it was an emotional statement. He was begging her, coaxing her, seducing her. And she was falling under the spell again, curling into the warmth of his male body, knowing he cared about her as much as she was beginning to care about him and realizing they were probably going to make love again. Only this time there'd be no mother clomping up the front steps to save her from explanations.

That one thought was two reasons to stop kissing him, and she did. She rose from the couch and paced away from him. Away from his warmth. Away from his scent. Away from his muffins. "Are you or are you not going to help me straighten this thing out with my parents?"

For a minute he just stared at her. Then he sighed and flopped back on the sofa, leaning his head against the pillow. "Caitlin . . ."

"Michael, if you don't want to help, just say no and I'll leave."

He dropped his hand to the couch cushion and looked as if he was going to press her for answers or explanations. Instead he sighed and gazed at the ceiling as though he knew she was a block of hot steel, untouchable, unbreakable. After a minute, he said, "Caitlin, what the hell can I possibly do?"

"Talk to him. You know, man talk."

"Why me?"

"He liked you. He was impressed with you."

"But I'm the one writing the story! He could hang me, shoot me, before I get a chance to get to the man talk."

"He blames Kiki because she's the one running around the neighborhood soliciting interviewees. He thinks Kiki's the nut who wants this dumb story and you're the one who's going to make my brother come out looking decent and moral."

"I get the picture," he said with a sigh.

Hearing the sound of reluctant agreement in his voice, she faced him and smiled hopefully. "Please?"

Nine

So, where do we find your dad?"

"You'll do it?"

He crossed his arms on his chest and studied her for a minute. "I guess. I'm not directly responsible for the controversy between your parents," he said as he rose from the couch, "but my article does seem to be the catalyst."

She couldn't argue with that.

"The whole purpose of this piece is to bring people together, yet the only thing I've accomplished is separating your parents."

"And Dad and Stash aren't talking, either."

"Great!" he mumbled as he stacked the coffee cups on the tray. "It's beginning to look like I'd be shirking my responsibilities if I didn't go and speak with your dad."

"Michael, that's all well and good, but don't be too surprised if my father...well, if he isn't exactly accommodating," she said for lack of a better word.

"In other words, he's furious."

"He's been cooking for himself since Monday."

"Great!" he said, and rolled his eyes. "Do you think we should call Bear? You know, ask him to come with us?"

She laughed. "No, I don't think we'll need Bear. I just wanted you to be prepared."

"Well, why didn't you just say that, instead of acting like your dad was a caged tiger looking for fresh meat?"

"Gee, I was only trying to help...."

He sighed with disgust, his male ego wounded because the lady in his life had inadvertently forced him to admit he wasn't Superman. "I've handled an irate father or two in my time, Caitlin."

"I'll just bet you have."

He heard it then. That subtle change of voice tone, the one he hadn't figured out yet, except to realize she was about to get nasty with him. He set the tray on the table. "Let's go," he said, changing his mind about the dishes and reaching down to grab her forearm. "Before you start slinging barbs again, let's just get our coats on and start across the river."

"Do you want to ride in my car?" she asked as they walked toward the elevator.

He pressed a button and a wall moved, exposing a closet of coats. He grabbed a jean jacket and pressed the button again. "It might look a little odd if we arrive in different cars. Unless you're not coming to this little chat."

"I don't know. Do you think I should?"

"Yes," he said, then started to laugh. "Your father might not be a caged tiger, but I'm not taking any chances. He'd never shoot me in front of a witness."

The elevator came, the doors swooshed open and they stepped inside. Even before they got to the ground floor, Caitlin realized that if she took him across the river in her car, she'd have to bring him back. Twenty minutes over. Twenty minutes back. After spending an afternoon listening to him befriending her father—doing her a favor—she'd have to spend another twenty minutes talking about it while they drove him home.

It was all too friendly. Too intimate.

"Maybe you ought to drive."

He looked over. "Huh?"

"I said I think you should drive."

For a minute he just stared at her. Then he shook his head. "That's right—if we go in the same car we'll be spending time together. Undoubtedly we'll laugh. We're good at that. We make each other happy. And after we make each other happy, we'll have that nice content feeling that so few people get to experience in their lives. Then we'll do a good deed together—talking to your dad. And that will strengthen the bond we're developing. Then we'll spend another twenty minutes alone in the car." He glanced over at her. "Being happy again. Lord knows, we couldn't let that happen."

"Will you please cut the sarcasm? You'd think you'd never been dumped before."

"Honey, I've been dumped! Just like you've obviously been dumped. We've all been dumped. But some of us don't let the experience make us cynical or jaded or just plain stupid!''

The elevator door swooshed open. He prodded her out the door by tapping her shoulder. "I've got to go back upstairs for my car keys."

They arrived at her parents' house at the same time. Traffic wasn't heavy on Sundays, so she suspected he took advantage of that and drove like a bat out of hell. His mood when he slammed his car door and stormed to the sidewalk confirmed that suspicion.

"Look, I'm sorry," Caitlin said. "I know I probably seem really dumb to you."

"Caitlin, I just can't figure you out. Why won't you at least explore this? We make each other happy. We're very physically attracted. Our backgrounds are different, but our morals are the same. Our values are the same. We're different enough to be interesting and enough alike to be compatible."

"Are you Catholic?"

"No, I'm Presbyterian."

"See, there's a difference right there."

He grabbed her arm and she stopped walking. "Cait, do you believe in God?"

"I don't see..."

"Do you believe in God?"

"Yeah."

"So do I. That makes us even. We just worship him a little differently. Neither one of us is exclusively right and neither one of us is totally wrong. Or would you take issue with that, too?"

She sighed. "No."

He motioned for her to precede him on the thin sidewalk. "Then please don't ever throw that up in my face again. You know as well as I do that differences like that can enrich your life, enhance it. Only fools let them become stumbling blocks."

She swallowed. "You're right."

She jogged up the porch steps, feeling properly chastised and unjustly chastised, because she felt the same way he did . . . again. As always. And she sensed he'd known all along she agreed with him and all he'd really done was call her bluff.

Caitlin opened the door and walked into the front hall. "Dad?" she called, walking toward the kitchen. "Dad?"

"You think he's home?" Michael asked as he leaned around her to peer into the dining room.

"I'll bet he's in the garage."

"Garage?"

"Yeah, he does woodworking. This fall he started building birdhouses. Drive down the back street sometime and look in the trees. My dad built every birdhouse."

"Generous, huh?"

"To a fault," Cait agreed and led Michael to the door in the kitchen. She opened it calling, "Dad?"

"Down here, Cait," he growled through a sigh.

"I brought Michael Flannery with me," she said as she began walking down the steps. Michael followed her.

The garage was small and warm, and rather than shelter a vehicle it housed a long worktable, which sat against a wall, and a jigsaw and a small mountain of wood, both of which were sort of dropped in the center.

"Flannery," Dad greeted as Michael walked down the steps.

"Hello, Mr. Petrunak."

"Dad," Cait began, "I told Michael about the troubles we've all been having because of his story—"

"What's he gonna do, send us to a counselor, too?"

Michael chuckled, deliberately keeping the tone light. "No. You guys don't need a counselor. In fact, I really don't understand what the big deal is here. I thought maybe if you explained it to me, there might be some way I could help."

"The big deal is that my wife, the woman I've supported for thirty-five years, walked out the door."

"She says you told her to get out," Caitlin bravely corrected him.

Dad snorted. "Sensitive. That's what she is. She knows I was just blowin' off steam and she took me literal...." He paused, frowned and said, "You know what I mean."

Michael instantly piped in with, "I know exactly what you mean. Just when you least expect it, a woman will turn on you, change on you." He watched Caitlin puttering around the room, obviously trying to ignore his innuendo and failing. "But you know what, Mr. Petrunak? There are times when I like that unpredictability."

"Ya better, if you're gonna be friends with Cait."

Michael noted the way Caitlin's dad had specifically emphasized the word "friends" and it struck him as odd, but he didn't have time to pursue it because he had other fish to fry. "Don't you sometimes like the idea that your wife's different from you? I mean, wouldn't it be dull if you married somebody just like yourself?''

"If Dad had married somebody just like himself, somebody stubborn, cantankerous and spoiled,'' Caitlin said with a giggle, "he'd either be dead or in jail for murder.''

"You watch your tongue,'' Dad said, but Michael was laughing, too.

"I think she's got a point, Mr. Petrunak.''

Dad turned to his worktable and eyed his row of paint cans. "Yeah, well...'' he sputtered.

"Oh, come on, Dad, admit it,'' Caitlin chortled. "Mom treats you very, very well.''

"And I'd be betting that you missed her this week,'' Michael added.

Dad grunted. "Missed her cooking.''

Michael chuckled. "And other things,'' he prodded, almost suggestively but not quite.

Dad glared at him. "Watch your mouth, young man.''

Caitlin sighed. "Dad, could you please...would you please go over to Mom and apologize?''

"I ain't done nothing wrong. She's the one who took what I said wrong.''

"But how was she supposed to know what you meant?'' Michael quickly asked. "I mean, you are the boss of the house, right? When you said get out, she got out.''

Dad's brow furrowed as he thought.

"The truth is,'' Michael added, "I think you hurt her feelings.''

Dad sighed. "I know I did.''

"But not on purpose," Michael said.

"No," Dad said, shaking his head. "Never on purpose." He sighed again. "I know Cait ain't gonna believe this, but I ain't never done anything to hurt that woman in thirty-five years. It's been eatin' away at me to think I did."

"So apologize," Cait prompted. Then she added, "We'll even come out with you for moral support."

Dad pulled off his gloves. "No. I'd rather go alone."

He'd no sooner made the announcement than he was walking toward the door. "Cait, make sure that saw's unplugged," he said as he walked out. "And if you leave the house," he added, "lock the front door. I've got my keys in my pocket."

For the first minute after he was gone the garage was stone silent. "Well, that was easy," Caitlin said in amazement. "I never, ever, expected him to so quickly admit he was wrong. I honestly thought we'd spend hours twisting his arm and finally end up begging him to go apologize."

Michael leaned on the table. "You certainly underestimate your father."

"Maybe."

"And his commitment to your mother."

"It's just that he's so... I don't know, bossy. He's so bossy that he always seems like he doesn't appreciate her."

"Has your mother ever complained?" he asked, watching her.

She paced to the other side of the garage. "No. And that used to make me really mad."

"It doesn't anymore."

She picked up an odd piece of wood, something cast aside but not thrown away, and she stared at it, obviously thinking deep thoughts. Then she said, "I've learned a lot in the last week."

"I did notice you were nicer, quieter, with your dad."

"Yeah, well, I just realized—I understood—what my mother was missing." She paused and drew a deep breath. "You know how it is. You don't think of your parents as being friends...or anything...and this week I saw my mother as a woman who was missing her man."

"It's interesting that you noticed that this particular week."

"It was hard not to, since she was living with me."

"And probably very hard not to after making love with me."

"You're getting arrogant again."

"Do you think I'm so stupid that I didn't notice you could handle the sex but not the intimacy? Cait, I'm nearly forty. I've slept with enough women to understand what happened between us."

She closed her eyes. "If you understand so well, then why don't you let me alone?"

"I don't want to leave you alone."

"Michael, I have problems—"

"I want to help you," he interrupted, because her tone was negative and desperate and it hurt him to hear the pain in her voice. "Whatever it is, we can overcome it. I know we can."

Before she could stop them, tears fell off her eyelids. "We can't."

He walked across the garage to stand in front of her and took her by the shoulders. "How do you know, when you won't try?" He folded her into his arms and hugged her. "If you need counseling, we'll go to counseling. I'll go with you. There isn't any problem...."

"Michael," she said, looking up at him. Big tears were splashing out of her eyes and her lips were trembling. "Michael," she whispered again. "I'm married."

Ten

It took a minute for that information to sink in. When it had, he said, "What?"

She swallowed. "I'm married."

"Where's your husband?" he asked, skeptical because she didn't act married and no one treated her as if she were married. Or did they? He took his hands off her shoulders.

"I don't know," she answered, walking away from him.

"You don't know?" he asked incredulously. "Do you mean, 'don't know' as in he deserted you? Or 'don't know' as in he's on a secret mission for the CIA? Or 'don't know' as in POW or MIA?"

"Michael, this is a long story and I . . ." She started crying again, long hard sobs that sounded as though they came from the depth of her soul.

"Let's go back to your apartment," Michael suggested, handing his hankie to her. She blew her nose and he almost dropped his arm across her shoulders, but he stopped himself. Yet, when he looked at her standing there sobbing into his hankie, he knew, just knew, he was supposed to be comforting her, loving her. "Better yet," he said, laying his arm across her shoulders to cuddle her to his side, "let's go back to my apartment. I know we have two cars—" he said, directing her toward the door leading to the driveway "—but I don't think you should drive. Let me, just this once, take care of you."

"I'm fine," she mumbled, then blew her nose again.

"You're not fine. You're like a mine field," Michael contradicted. "Any minute you're going to blow apart, and when you do I want to be there to pick up the pieces."

"I'm fine," she insisted, shrugging out of his hold. She was trembling. Her shoulders drooped and her knees seemed to be wobbling.

"In a pig's eye," he said and scooped her off her feet.

She cried through the entire drive across the river, cried in the elevator the whole way from the basement parking garage to the penthouse. She cried as he helped her off with her coat, cried when he put it away, cried while he decided where they should talk and continued to cry as he led her to his bedroom, sat her on the bed and slipped off her loafers.

He pulled the fat pillows from under the spread and leaned them against the headboard, then directed her to sit, legs extended, resting against the pillows. Then he rounded the bed, took off his tennies and slid beside her, putting his arm around her shoulders.

"I want the whole story," he said quietly.

"It is long. It is stupid. And it is really hard for me to talk about it."

"Well, I think you need to talk about it."

She sniffed and he grabbed the box of tissues from his bedside table. "Here, gimme that hankie. I think it's served its time. We'll go with the tissues from here on out." He wiped the tears from her cheeks. "There. Now, shoot."

"I'd like to. When I look back, I'd really like to."

"Then just start at the beginning."

She sighed. "Okay."

Several minutes passed in a silence punctuated only by the sound of Caitlin blowing her nose. Once she sighed. Twice she tried to talk, but nothing came out. Finally, in a low, shaky voice she said, "I dated my husband, oh, from, I think, sophomore year in high school. But you know how that is. You're dating this week and not dating next. And seeing each other in school more than anywhere else."

"Your dad approved of this."

She laughed. "No. But that just made it all the more romantic. You know, sneaking out of the house and stuff."

"Uh-huh," he said. "Go on."

"Anyway, I was allowed to date my senior year, so Ted and I, you know, actually went steady. I got his class ring and all that jazz, and we really thought we were in a relationship. At least, *I* thought it was a relationship." She snorted with disgust. "Boy, did I have a lot to learn."

"So, when did you get married?"

"This is the really great part," she said, and then her breath shuddered out on a sigh as her crying seemed to slow to a crawl. "We got married two weeks before college started." She paused and when she spoke again, her voice was back to being a slow, shaky whisper. "My dad didn't really want me to go to college. He said women were supposed to get married. And he never missed the opportunity to tell me I was wasting my time getting a fancy education that I'd never use because once I got pregnant I'd have to quit working. He never really understood...."

She quieted again, this time leaning against the pillows with a heavy sigh. Michael tightened his arm around her shoulders. "Never really understood what?"

She closed her eyes. "He never really understood that the more he hassled me about going to college, the more determined I was to get there."

"That's typical. The minute a parent tells a kid they can't do something is the minute the kid figures out a way to do it."

"Yeah, well, I didn't have to figure out a way."

He sighed. "I have a feeling I'm going to hate this, but tell me anyway."

"Deep down, I really didn't want to disobey my father. I wanted to do what he wanted me to do, get married, have kids...grandkids that he could bounce on his knee...but I also wanted to go to college. And I was mad that he was interfering." She paused again and took a long breath.

"One day—it was a Sunday—I was sitting on the front porch with Ted's mother, telling her my troubles, about how my dad infuriated me, yet somehow or another I still felt like I was disobeying him. About then, Ted's father came out of the house and sat on the front step, listening. When I ran out of steam, Ted's parents kind of looked at each other funny. Then his mother made the suggestion that if Ted and I got married, I could please everybody—with the exception that we'd have to postpone having kids. But it would be like a show of good faith to my father. Proof that I wouldn't change just because I got an education."

"How old was Ted?"

"We were the same age."

"Was he working?"

"No, he was going to go to college too."

"So how were two college kids going to support themselves?"

"We were going to live with Ted's parents."

"And who was going to pay your tuition?"

"Ted's parents paid his. I had a scholarship."

"Oh, okay, it makes sense."

"It made wonderful sense. Ted was the man in my life. The only man who'd ever been in my life, and in those days that was what you did. You married the guy you dated all through high school."

"So when did it go sour?"

"It didn't go sour, because it never really existed."

"You lost me."

"Well, we planned a really traditional wedding. Just the way everybody else did. And even though my parents were a little, um, I don't know, unhappy maybe, they didn't really say much because it was normal for people to get married after high school, except the guy would go to work in the mill and the girl would stay home and have babies."

"So you were typical, but you weren't really typical because you were going to college rather than the other stuff. You sort of countered every argument they had."

"Yeah," she said, nodding, happy that he seemed to understand. "Okay, so, we had this showboat wedding and a big bridal dance and a little honeymoon at Virginia Beach and then we came home and took over his room at his parents' house and began college. But the strangest thing happened...."

She trailed off and closed her eyes again and Michael waited, and waited, and waited. Finally he said, "What?"

"We...I can't explain it except to say we saw less of each other married than we ever had single."

"Sounds like a pretty typical marriage to me," he said, then chuckled. "Just trying to bring a little humor to this."

"It's really not funny. It was a nightmare. We'd go to school, I'd come home and help his mother with dinner, then we'd eat, and then Ted would disappear while I'd study. His parents would go to bed at about ten. I'd generally study until about twelve and then I'd go to bed, never really knowing when he'd come home. On bad nights he'd wake me to make love."

They were both quiet, both simply breathing, as he soaked in that much of her story and she remembered. Some good things. Some bad things.

"Most of it was bad," she said suddenly. "He'd come home drunk or high or both. Sometimes he'd throw up and I'd be the one to clear away the evidence. I worked very hard to protect him, to keep his parents from finding out. Turns out they knew. They'd always known...."

"They wanted you to marry him to get him off the street, didn't they?"

"Yeah. But you see, I didn't know that. I didn't even suspect what he was really like. While we were dating, he'd drop me off at my house with a good-night kiss and wave and I'd think he was going home. But he never, ever, went home before three, and sometimes he stayed out all night ... roaming around on *your* side of the river. That's why I never found out. And his parents didn't even hint about any of this until the day he left for good."

"Where did he go?"

"We have no idea. None of us. He wrote twice to get money and both times it was from a different address, but he never came home."

"Did you send him money?"

"He never asked me. He wrote to his parents and they sent him the money."

"Just like they always did."

She nodded. "Exactly. Ultimately, I divorced him because one of the times he asked for money, it was for bail. God knows what he'd been accused of. His parents never told me. But a counselor at school advised me to divorce him so I wouldn't be held liable for anything he did."

"I thought you said you were still married?"

"In the eyes of the church I am."

Slowly, other things she'd said found their meaning and after a minute he said, "Which is one of the ways we're different."

"Right."

"And you could never go against the rules of your church?"

"No."

"Ever think of joining mine?"

She laughed. "I'd love to be able to join another church, to think that it would be that easy to get myself out of this mess, but I can't. While I was still in college, still young—still open to suggestion, so to speak—I thought I could eventually do that, but as I grew older I realized being Catholic is as much a part of me as being Irish or having green eyes. I can't explain it, except to say that it hurt me more to give up my faith than it did to lose my husband."

"You probably should have shot your husband."

She laughed again, then bit her lower lip. "That's also against my religion. Yours, too."

He sighed. "At this minute, I'm a little tempted to test that rule."

"Well, you'd have to find Ted first."

"Have you ever tried?"

"I hired a private investigator once."

"And?"

"And he found nothing. My husband began changing his name after his first arrest and the investigator connected him to at least eight, but after that the trail grew cold. He never used his real name again. He never used the same alias twice. He doesn't want to be found and we won't find him."

Michael blew his breath out on a sigh. "That makes it tough.

"So," he said, bringing back the original topic, "did you ever try to annul your marriage? I don't know much about this, but I do know some Catholics can get an annulment through the church.''

Michael watched Caitlin's eyes pool with tears and he almost wished he would have saved that question for another time because she'd been through enough already. "I tried," she said, and closed her eyes. "When my in-laws kicked me out for not fulfilling my responsibilities as a good wife to their son—"

"Oh, God." Michael groaned. "You're kidding."

"No, they threw my clothes out on the street and screamed at me, threatening to call the police if I wasn't off their property in ten minutes."

"Oh, God, you poor kid. How old were you?"

"Still eighteen. My marriage lasted about ten months. That's it."

"And you can't get it annulled?"

"It was consummated. I made the commitment in good faith. From my point of view, I'm locked in."

Just from the way she emphasized good-faith commitment and point of view, Michael realized that was the key. She'd locked herself in by being honest, so the answer somehow lay with her husband, the half of the partnership that wasn't good. "What about your husband's commitment?"

"Well, right before they threw me on the street, my in-laws told me that they'd threatened Ted with some kind of punishment if he didn't settle down. And they figured getting him married to this nice little Catholic girl was the best way to settle him down. So it wasn't Ted's idea to marry me. It was his parents'."

"Then he didn't make a commitment."

"No. He did not."

"And if you could find him, you could probably get the marriage annulled."

"I could definitely get the marriage annulled. I'd talked to a priest and he told me that if Ted's parents would simply admit they coerced him into marrying me, I could easily get an annulment."

"But Ted's parents refused to do that."

"Right again. They pretended they had no idea what I was talking about whenever Father Connelly went to speak with them, and that made my testimony look like a lie."

"But why?" Michael asked, exasperated, infuriated and just plain confused. "What had you ever done to them to deserve that?"

"It wasn't a question of what I'd done to them, because I hadn't ever done anything to them. It was more a matter of keeping their son's good name intact."

"His good name?" Michael gasped. "Caitlin, get real. He didn't have a good name."

Caitlin sighed. "Michael, he did his running on the other side of the river. No one but me and his parents ever had any inkling of what he was really like."

"And no one believes you? Or is it that you've chosen not to tell anyone?"

"Let's put it this way—everybody I've told believes me. I just haven't told a whole heck of a lot of people."

"So your ex-husband really does have a good name, doesn't he?"

She thought about that. Before she spoke, she looked at the ceiling. "At first, his parents spread the story that he left to get away from me. But somehow or another the bail-money story got around. I'm not sure how. Stash said Ted's father got drunk and blurted it . . . I don't know. Anyway, time kind of cleared my name."

"To everybody but the church."

She sighed. "Rules are rules, Michael."

He combed his fingers through his hair. "Caitlin, how in the hell can you be so calm about this?"

She laughed shakily. "I've just been crying for the last two hours. I don't call this calm." She took a deep breath. "But I was calm, rational . . . maybe resigned is a better word . . . until I met you."

Neither said a word for a minute or so, and then Michael noticed she'd grown stiff and still, that she was imperceptibly pulling away from him.

"I make you wish you could get married again?" he asked quietly, cautiously.

She laughed and he felt her relax a little. "You are so vain," she said, tapping his forearms to chastise him.

"Then what?" he asked, confused again.

"You just . . . remind me of . . . stuff."

"What stuff?" he asked, twisting to face her.

"Stuff I'd just rather not talk about."

"Sex?"

"Will you stop!"

"No, tell me," he said, peering down so that he could see her face.

"I absolutely refuse to tell you."

"You absolutely have to tell me," he insisted, still peeking at her curiously. "I feel like I am a great big part of pulling you out of your problem. I've felt since the minute I met you that there was something about

you that involved me and if you don't tell me everything—"

"Not on your life."

He frowned. "Cait, how am I going to help you if
you won't tell me how I fit in?"

"You don't fit in. As far as I'm concerned, this is
between me, my ex-husband and my church," she said
with an exasperated sigh. "There isn't anything you or
anybody else can do to get me out of it. Don't try. I
don't want you to try."

"Whoa, whoa," he said, holding up his hand to
stop her ranting. "You're doing it again. Just like after we made love. You're throwing up imaginary bar-
riers, convincing yourself while you pretend to be
convincing me that you don't care. That you don't
want help. That you're strong enough to handle this
alone. Well, I'm telling you you don't have to. I want
to help you."

"And I'm telling you you can't help me."

"I could try, if you'd keep going with your story."

"There is no rest of the story."

"There's the part about how I fit in," he reminded
her again, slowly, cautiously.

She shook her head and slid away from him. "You
won't have a minute's peace until I tell you this," she
said, moving her legs across the bed and then putting
her feet on the floor. "So I'm going to tell you," she
added as she rose.

"This embarrasses you," he observed out loud,
though he hadn't intended to.

"Of course it embarrasses me!" she said, then
laughed shakily.

He crossed his arms on his chest and studied her. "Why?"

"Why?" she asked, and laughed again. "Because it was bad enough that I found you attractive. Now I have to admit that you were sort of irresistible."

"I like that in a woman," Michael said, grinning.

She sighed. "I figured you would," she said, and began looking around for her shoes.

She stooped beside the bed, resting her arm along the edge as she peeked underneath for her loafers. He caught her arm. She glanced at his hand, then looked him right in the eyes.

He smiled. "I'm not buying it."

She arched both eyebrows. "I've never known you to pass up a compliment."

"Oh, I don't think I'd be passing up a compliment. I think that when you get down to the truth, the real nitty-gritty—" with each word his voice got softer and he inched closer to her face until their lips were almost touching "—it'll probably be very, very complimentary."

She touched his cheek with two fingers, tracing the line of his beard. "You make me laugh."

"See, I knew it'd be good. Go on."

"You make me mad."

"You make me mad sometimes," he countered with a chuckle.

She caught his gaze and held it, her fingers still resting on his cheek. "Don't you see?" she said, then bit her lower lip. "You make me feel. I'm not supposed to feel...."

"Sometimes you can't stop it, Cait," he said, understanding what he said even as he said it. He caught her fingers. "What are you going to do? Go through life pretending you don't have feelings?"

She smiled sadly. "I was doing a damned good job until I met you." She sighed, shaking her head. "I work with men. I know every man who drinks at Catz. And in all this time, not one has ever..."

He leaned closer. "Ever what?"

She licked her lips. "Ever..."

He leaned closer still. "Ever?"

"Made me feel..."

"Like?"

She closed her eyes and took a deep breath. "No one's ever made me feel like a woman," she whispered, then opened her eyes. "There. Happy?" she asked, almost defiantly. "Now you know. All these years, I've lived this strange, strange life. I never really felt like a woman, just a person. And you make me long for something I know I can never have. Not sex. But intimacy, identity." She closed her eyes. "I want to be a woman again. I like being a woman."

Eleven

When Michael walked into his office the next morning Kiki was waiting for him. "Get out," he snarled. "I'm not in the mood for anybody this morning, but you I'd like to kill."

"I love you, too, Mikey," she said, then pulled his tall-back chair away from his desk. She patted it twice. "Come on, sit. Tell me what happened."

"Kiki, get out."

She patted his chair again. "Sit."

He sighed.

"Sit. I'm not leaving till you tell me what's wrong, so sit."

He stormed across the room, threw his briefcase on the desk and then sat. "Caitlin is divorced. She refuses to see me anymore. I refuse to do your story. Now get out."

"Like her a lot, don't you?" Kiki asked mischievously.

"If I didn't like her so much, I wouldn't give a damn that she refuses to see me. Get out!"

"I knew it! I knew it! The minute she strolled into that bar I said, 'There she is. That's the one.'"

He swiveled his chair around and grabbed the front of her blouse, bending her toward him. "What?"

She grinned. "I think you understood me."

"You mean there never was a story?"

"Well, there is now."

"You set me up?"

"And then had to run all over creation making trouble so you or Caitlin would be forced to—"

"You nearly broke up a marriage!"

"You fixed it!"

He dropped his head back and groaned. "I'm calling your mother."

"I'm sure she'll be pleased to hear that I finally set you up with the woman of your dreams."

"Oh, you set me up, all right," he said, turning his chair around again as she walked to a seat in front of his desk. "Kiki, Cait's divorced. A divorced Catholic. She doesn't want to get involved again. She wants...chooses...to remain single."

Kiki frowned. "That's weird."

Michael sighed. "She's very committed to her roots. You have to know her to understand. But the bottom line is that she wants to remain Catholic. Even dating me is out of the question. Marrying me is impossible."

"Can't she get an annulment?"

"No." He sighed. "Look, I probably shouldn't be telling you this stuff, but she could get an annulment if her in-laws would testify that they forced their son to marry her."

"Why doesn't her ex-husband just testify?"

"No one knows where he is."

"So find him."

She said it so quickly, so easily, that Michael stared at her.

"You're supposed to be such a crackerjack reporter," she taunted. "Find him."

"Caitlin would never let me go pok—"

"Don't tell her."

"What?"

"Find him on your own. Find out where he is and why he left and make the pitch for him to do Cait a favor. That way if there's a real ugly problem you can protect her until you get this mess cleared up."

He started to chuckle, then his chuckle turned into a laugh, then his laugh turned into hysteria. "You're crazy."

"No," Kiki said as she rose. "You're crazy. All you have to do is find one guy, get him to sign a few papers. It's just a question of whether or not you really want to." She strolled to the door. "If she gets her annulment, it's wedding bells for you, ya know? And I think that's the real problem here. See ya."

He sat back in his chair, watching her skip down the hall. Then he crossed his arms on his chest and looked at the ceiling.

It was Friday before Caitlin felt stable enough to go to work, but she'd taken the entire week off so she stayed home anyway, figuring the extra day, plus the weekend, couldn't hurt. She'd never been so traumatized in her whole life, never wanted something so badly she thought she'd die without it. She'd been tempted before. She'd had sad days and known loneliness. But never had the instinct to marry, mother children and grow old with someone swelled inside her to the point she couldn't control it. She wasn't really sure she could control it now and that's why she made Michael promise he'd stay away from her. Forever. For good. Anything else was tempting fate.

She made coffee, let Ernest in, watched him lob his way to the back bedroom and then turned on the TV set. The woman on the morning news was a mother whose child had chicken pox and the cast and crew were laughing about it. Caitlin frowned, took a deep breath and rose from the couch. On her way to the kitchen, she smacked the knob on the television set, silencing the laughter.

She poured herself a mug of coffee and sipped it while she leaned against the counter. The problem was, she decided, now that she'd established herself at Barnhart Steel, the fun had gone out of her work and what she needed to do was get another job. A more stimulating job. Or maybe a job that would make her feel as though she was doing something really worthwhile. That was it. She needed to do something worthwhile. And she knew just how to find a worthwhile project. She'd go and see Father Connelly.

Satisfied with that decision, she poured her coffee down the drain and headed for her bedroom. Before she even reached the hall, the phone rang.

"How are ya today, Cait?" It was her father.

"Good. Really good," she said, sighing a little. "I decided that I need something in my life. Maybe some volunteer work, maybe to do the books for a struggling sole proprietor. So, I'm on my way to see Father Connelly."

"That's a good idea, Cait," her father agreed enthusiastically. "Drop by here after you talk to him and let your mother and me know—"

"Not yet, Dad," she quickly refused, though she was kind about it. "I'm just not ready yet."

"You go see Father Connelly," Stan said quietly. "Your mother and I'll be here when you need us."

"I know," she whispered, nodding her head. "I'll see ya, okay?"

"Okay," he said and hung up.

Caitlin drew a deep breath and turned toward the bedroom again. She couldn't seem to disassociate her parents and Michael. It wasn't just because they'd been together or because they were involved with Michael's story. Every time she looked at her parents, happily growing old together, sharing secrets they kept even from their children, she thought of Michael, of what she'd be missing, and the strangest urge to cry would creep up on her. It was then that she picked up her pace and almost ran to her bedroom. She changed sweaters, brushed her hair and slid into boots.

At the door she grabbed her old stadium coat, shoved her hands into her black leather gloves and rummaged through her purse for her sunglasses. It had snowed the night before and the bright sun was bouncing off the layers of sparkling white snow. The sunglasses were a necessity to keep from going blind. She wasn't hiding...she really wasn't. With that thought she took a scarf from her purse and tied it under her chin. Then she pulled her door shut and jogged down the steps.

She ran to the church and tapped on the rectory door. No answer. Crunching fresh snow in the small section between the rectory and Father Connelly's garage, she made her way to a window and peeked in. No car.

She sighed, tossing her head back in a sad sort of despair, glancing up at the bright sun in the blue sky. How could a day that looked so beautifully right be so terrible? She sighed again and stared at the tall, pointy steeple, with its simple silver cross glistening in the sun. The wind burned her cheek and caught the tail of her scarf, waving it and making a loud flapping noise. The cold air dried her nostrils.

She looked at the steeple. Looked at the beautiful blue sky. Looked at the building that had stood proud and strong for over a hundred years.

The wind whipped her scarf again.

She could go in.

It wouldn't hurt.

Couldn't hurt.

She sighed and headed for the huge double doors.

Inside it wasn't much warmer than outside, but the wind wasn't blowing. She removed her glasses and stuffed them in her purse as she walked through the vestibule to the swinging door that led to the seats and altar. She'd always wondered if there was a name for this part. If the front was the vestibule and the back was the sacristy, then what was the middle? She'd always wanted to ask.

She pushed open the door and cautiously crept up the wide middle aisle. Every step of her high-heeled boots echoed around her. In its cavernous stillness there was a calm, a tranquillity, about the church she'd never noticed before. She took a few more steps up the center aisle, remembering the swoosh of her wedding dress, the happy faces of the crowd, Father Connelly beaming from the head of the church, waiting for her...and Ted in a tux. Poor Ted. If she considered herself to have been taken for a fool, then Ted had been trapped, imprisoned. She was much too smart to hate him, much too smart to think the blame should be his alone. But how could anybody be angry with an eighteen-year-old girl with stars in her eyes and big dreams?

Tears welled in her eyes and she bit her bottom lip.

What she wouldn't give for one more chance....

"Cait?"

"Michael!" Her whisper was loud and it echoed around her. Stupidly, she said, "Shh."

He began walking up the center aisle to meet her. "What are you doing here?"

"What are *you* doing here?"

He grinned and spread his hands. "I asked first."

"I'm here to see Father Connelly."

"That's what your dad said. So I went to the rectory but there's nobody there."

"No kidding."

"Look, could we talk?"

She shook her head, remembering the last time they were together. In his bedroom. Snuggling on a bed. Intimately sharing secrets. That had been her breaking point. The physical attraction was one thing. The

friendship was another. Put them together and ...
forget it. "I don't think so."

He glanced around. "I'd be willing to talk here. If
we're allowed ... to talk, that is."

She sighed. "I taught a catechism class in this
church, right up there." She turned, pointing to the
front right-hand corner.

"Then we're allowed to talk in here."

"It isn't prison," she said defensively.

"I know that," he whispered. "And I certainly
didn't mean to imply anything bad. I was just making
sure...." He rubbed the back of his neck. "How about
sitting?" he asked quietly, and there was such a
strange expression on his face that Caitlin slowly
moved into a pew. He paced in front of her. Once up.
Once back. Then he turned. "Cait, your ex-husband
is dead."

For a minute the muscles of her face were totally
frozen. Then she said, "Dead?"

"He's been dead for three years."

"Three years?" she asked, stupefied. "I don't understand."

Michael hunkered down by the armrest of her pew.
"He was killed in a drug bust...in Colorado." He took
a deep breath and closed his eyes. "His parents knew."

Her lips trembled, so she pressed them together. "It
figures."

He rubbed her knuckles with his index finger. "I'm
sorry."

"So am I." She glanced at her gloved hand, where
his index finger cautiously made contact. "He never
had much of a chance to live."

"Cait, he did exactly what he wanted to do. He also shot a policeman before the vice guy shot him."

She squeezed her eyes shut. "Oh, God."

"I'm surprised his parents could keep this quiet. They must either have money or friends in high places...."

"Both."

He waited for her to elaborate and then realized she wasn't going to. "You okay?"

She nodded, but despite her best efforts to stop them her lips trembled violently. Big tears splashed off her cheeks.

"You want a glass of water or anything?"

She shook her head.

"Do you want me to go?"

She shook her head again.

"Then can I sit, too?"

She nodded and slid over on the seat as Michael slipped in beside her. She slumped forward, sobbing into her hands, and he reached over and gathered her to him, nestling her face into his shoulder. He had absolutely no idea of what she was feeling and therefore no idea of what to say, so he just held her, stroking her hair. The sun poured in through the stained-glass windows and made colored circles on the varnished wood pews and he watched it, watched the dust dance in the colored light.

Her crying slowed, then stopped completely, but she didn't move. She was still for so long he wondered if she'd fallen asleep. He slid down a little bit to get more comfortable himself and closed his eyes. The big empty church was peaceful and quiet and he felt as though he was far, far away from civilization...or maybe on a different planet.

"You can go if you like," she whispered into his shoulder.

"I'm fine."

"I ruined your topcoat."

"My parents are rich. I'll get a new one."

She laughed softly.

Another minute passed in silence. Then she said, "Thank you."

He whispered, "Your welcome," and kissed her hair.

She snuggled against him with an after-crying sigh and he closed his eyes again. "I've known since Tuesday," he confessed quietly.

He felt her swallow. "I sort of thought so. I don't suppose that kind of information is too difficult to find if you know where to look. I'm only surprised it took you until Tuesday."

"I didn't start looking until Tuesday."

"Oh."

He let another minute tick off the clock. "I wasn't sure how you'd react to the news that Ted was dead."

"I have always and will always feel sorry for him."

"I can't believe you're not angry."

"I am angry...sort of. I guess maybe disgusted is a better word. But when I think about it I realize I didn't really lose anything."

"I don't understand," he said, and slid his hand up and down the sleeve of her stadium coat.

"Well, his parents protected me by hiding this information," she said softly. "I had a lot of time to get over a bad marriage, a lot of time to think about my mistakes. A lot of time to decide what I really wanted out of life."

"And what's that?"

She pushed herself away from him, sitting up so she could look at his face as she spoke. "I think I want a tall, handsome husband who can cook. But the only guy I know who fits that bill took days before he got up the courage to tell me my first husband was dead."

"And don't forget the day it took me before I got up the nerve to begin investigating at all."

She looked him in the eye. "Why did you investigate?"

"Because I want to marry you."

"Oh, I really believe that." She smiled. "You knew this stuff Tuesday and it's Friday. I somehow find it hard to believe that you helped me so you could marry me."

"Would you believe I got cold feet?"

She shook her head. "You?"

"Yeah. I'm sorry."

"Oh, don't be sorry," she said, motioning for him to stand so they could leave. "I'm beginning to think getting cold feet before a wedding is probably wise."

He rose and stepped into the aisle. "Do you really want to marry me?" he asked, and tried to put his arm around her but she bobbed down on one knee and made the sign of the cross. "What's that?"

"Genuflecting. A sign of respect."

"Show me."

"Well," she said, pulling him to stand by the pew. "Most people stay close to the seat so they can use it to balance themselves, like this," she said, and took his hand and laid it on the armrest. "Now you go down on your right knee. Since you're not Catholic, you can just bow your head."

He did that, then grabbed her hand. "While I'm down here," he said, smiling, "I have a request."

Confused, she whispered, "What's that?"

"Will you marry me?"

"You're determined to get an answer this morning, aren't you?"

"Yes. So say you'll marry me."

"On one condition."

He frowned. "What?"

She tugged on his hand to get him to stand. "That you let Stash alone. Honestly, Michael," she said, slipping her hand in the crook of his arm as they walked out of the church. "The kid knows what he wants and your Myranda has him thinking about forestry. Forestry, of all things."

"He has the right to get his options," Michael said, and pushed open the swinging door.

Caitlin stepped through but turned and glanced up at the altar. She got the strangest feeling, almost as though someone had called her. But there was no one on the altar. No one in the church. She took another step but again stopped and looked around.

Standing with one of the two swinging doors in his hand, Michael smiled and shook his head. "Just say thanks."

She glanced at him. "You won't think I'm silly?"

"I'll always think you're silly. But I already said thanks, so He must be waiting for you."

She turned, waved and whispered, "Thanks," then took Michael's arm again. "Want to get married in the summer?"

"I want to get married in the winter. Preferably this winter."

"That's a little soon.... What about kids?"

"I've always wanted four."

She frowned. "Better plan on a couple more. Catholics use natural family planning."

This time he frowned. "What's that?"

"Rhythm. Temperature taking, calendar watching—or just lots of kids."

"But your parents only have two kids," he pointed out as they walked arm in arm toward the heavy double doors.

"My mother had a difficult time getting pregnant, but everybody else in her family was a regular fertility machine."

"Oh, Lord, what am I getting into?"

She grabbed his arm and stopped him just as they got to the main doors. "Are you sure this is what you want?"

He saw the time for teasing was over and took her by the shoulders. "I'm rich. We can have thirty kids. That's really not an issue. I love you, Cait. I spent the last few days alone proving to myself what the rest of my life would be like without you, and do you know what?"

She shook her head.

"It's pretty boring." He dropped his arm on her shoulders and pushed open the huge wooden doors. "Let's go look at your calendar."

She stopped walking again. "Why?"

"Why what?" he asked, sounding confused.

"Why do you want to look at my calendar?"

He pulled her from the vestibule of the church into the sunny winter day and let the door close behind them. "To see if it's okay to . . . you know," he said, gesturing with his hands.

"Make love?" she asked, surprised that he seemed to be stumbling.

"Yes, Caitlin," he said. "Make love. We'll see if it's okay—you know, make sure that you won't get pregnant."

He began to walk away but she grabbed his arm. "Michael, at this point that's really not a consideration."

"Caitlin, at this point, since we're not married, it's probably our most important consideration."

Smiling wryly, she shook her head once.

His jaw drooped. "Don't even say it," he warned her quietly. "Don't even think it."

"Michael, making love once can be considered getting carried away with the moment, but this is premeditated. I can't."

He squeezed his eyes shut. "Cait, are you trying to tell me that not only are you going to make me wait six or eight months, maybe even a year, to get married, but we're going to remain celibate while we wait?"

"I know that probably seems idealistic to you, but stop and think, Michael. I was celibate for ten years."

He tossed his head back and groaned. "Cait!"

Twelve

M arried for two hours and you're already staring at another man."

They were waltzing and he whirled her once in a looping circle as they glided around the grand ballroom of the Onyx Hotel.

"Sorry," Caitlin said, and looked up at Michael with a smile. Pearls sparkled in her bright hair and her ivory satin dress picked up the multicolored lights by the bandstand and reflected them. "I just can't believe my father's in a tux."

"I can't believe your father gets along with my father. Nobody gets along with my father."

"I love your father."

He bent and kissed the tip of her nose. "You love everybody."

When he straightened, she was gazing at him in that soft, feminine way she had, the innocent look that sank into his bones and just turned him into jelly. "How long till that bridal dance?"

"Only another two or three hours."

"Two or three hours?" he groaned, then whirled her around again. "I obviously didn't know what I was doing when I let your father talk us into a big wedding."

"We could skip out." She smiled. "For the next two hours all we really do is mingle with guests. If we disappeared right now it would be an hour before anybody actually missed us because everybody would just assume we were mingling on the other side of the room and vice versa."

He nodded his head in the direction of their proud fathers as the two men moved from one cluster of guests to another. "Your dad would have a conniption."

"Not if we didn't tell him," she said as she traced the line of Michael's jaw, then let her fingers slide down his neck, along his shirt collar and across the lapel of his tuxedo jacket.

"You mean you want to just walk out the door without telling anybody?"

"Precisely." She stood on her tiptoes and lightly kissed his mouth. Once, twice. Then she freed her hand from his and put both arms around his neck and pressed herself against him. "You did reserve a room here, didn't you?"

A wave of people danced by and Michael realized they were in the center of the dance floor, secluded from the rest of the world by intense waltzers. "Yes, I did,'' he said, and swallowed. "And if you don't back off about a pace and stop tickling my neck, I'm simply going to pick you up and carry you upstairs. To hell with the elevator."

She giggled. "Actually, I think I'd like that."

He closed his eyes and grimaced. "Please do not tease me. I just barely made it through the two months of waiting to get married, but I made it. Let me get through the last two hours with dignity."

"Let's get through the next two hours in our room, drinking champagne." She rose to her tiptoes and kissed him again. "Please?"

He opened his eyes. "You're not teasing, are you?"

She shook her head.

He didn't give her the chance to change her mind. Instead, he put his hands on her wrists, pulling her close enough that their noses bumped. Then he whispered, "If anybody stops us to chat, we're on our way for a drink because we're *really* thirsty. There isn't a person in this crowd who'd detain a thirsty man."

She grinned at him. "How devious you're getting."

"When a person has the right motive, he can plan just about any crime."

"What do we tell people when we get to the door?"

He jutted his chin in the direction of the ballroom entrance. The big double doors were open and the lobby was in view. "There are people milling in the halls. We'll just mingle our way to the elevator."

"And if somebody catches us getting into an elevator and decides to chase us?" she asked, then giggled.

"They have no idea what room we're in, Mrs. Jankowski."

"Oh, you devil!" she shrieked, and laughed with delight. "This is perfect."

He took her hand and turned her in the direction of the double doors. "Just continue to smile and complain a lot about being thirsty but above all keep walking."

"Got it," she said, and straightened her shoulders.

It went more quickly and more easily than Caitlin would have believed, and before she knew it they were alone in a velvet-walled elevator. The second the door swished closed he pulled her into his arms and kissed her.

"How long has it been since I told you that I love you?"

"All of thirty seconds."

"Too long," he said, and kissed her again.

The bell rang, the doors opened and they continued to kiss. When the door began to close, Michael stuck out his foot to prevent it but finished his kiss before he actually made a move to get out.

In the hall he took her hand and pulled her behind him, glancing at the room numbers as they went. All of a sudden he stopped and scooped her off her feet.

"What are you doing?" she asked, giggling, as he jostled her to get a better hold.

"Carrying you over the threshold," he said, and shifted her again. "Grab the key from my breast pocket."

"Okay," she said, and slid her hand into the pocket of his tuxedo, feeling for the key but not finding it.

He cleared his throat. "A little more quickly, please."

Caitlin smiled. "Oh, don't you like that?" she asked, and rubbed her fingers along the inside of his pocket again.

"Caitlin, I love that, but there are a lot of other things I love even better, and honestly, I think you've tormented me enough. Grab the key, open that door and let me make love to you until we both collapse from exhaustion."

She started to laugh but did as he said. Once they were inside their room, she dropped the key into his pocket again and he looked at her long and hard, in a way that almost made her blush; then he kissed her. When he finally pulled away and eased his arms down so she could slide to the floor, the only sound in the room was the rustle of her satin dress against the smooth material of his black tux.

She couldn't stop staring at him. "You look very handsome in a tux."

"You look very beautiful in a wedding dress."

"No regrets?"

"None. Absolutely none," he said as he bent to kiss her again. She stretched to meet him, pushing herself to her tiptoes so she could enjoy every second of a very long, sensuous kiss. Then she felt his fingers at the zipper of her wedding dress and she slipped her hands to his tie.

He pulled her zipper to her buttocks just as she unraveled his tie, and they stepped away from each other long enough for Michael to slide the crisp satin down her arms. Pulling his tie from his collar, Caitlin stepped out of the dress. She grasped its lacy shoulder and tossed it to an available chair, even as Michael took her waist and pulled her close again. As the dress fell in a soft puff of shiny ivory, their lips met in a long, lingering kiss. Then she began unbuttoning his shirt and he slid the straps of her lacy slip off her shoulders. She pulled away from him again and her sheer garment tumbled to the floor.

"I'll get that," he said, and bent to grab the slip. He tossed it to the chair, and when he faced her she noticed he was unbuttoning his shirt.

She drew close again, sliding her arms around his waist, under the cool silk of his shirt, then stretching to kiss him. He rubbed his hands down her back, over her hips and then up again. When he reached the clasp of her bra, he put his knee on the bed and pulled her down to lie with him.

The only light in the room was a small lamp by the door, but when she removed Michael's shirt his skin seemed to burn with an orangish flame, and when she touched him he was warmer than she expected. She watched her hand glide over his skin, weaving her fingers through the rich black hair on his chest.

The low light seemed to flicker, giving the room a magical quality, and Caitlin continued to watch her hand as she smoothed her palm across his flesh, not just touching him but experiencing him, loving him. The light grew bright and everything in the room began to shimmer and sparkle; then a tear rolled to her eyelashes and fell on her cheek and the light became normal again. She closed her eyes and collapsed to her back. The light wasn't changing; she was crying. She was making the magic with her tears.

She would have given in to it, would have cried long and hard and told him the secrets of her soul, but he began kissing her, running his lips along the line of her torso, across her belly and to her thighs. Her tears stopped and she lay still, completely taken by the tingling sensations as they combined with the sweet emotion of the moment. The freedom of intimacy was a wonderful, beautiful gift, something to be treasured and cherished and never taken for granted. And he was telling her that. Not with words but with deeds. With love and trust and something akin to reverence, he was expressing her very thoughts.

"Come here," he whispered, pulling her up to lay her head on the pillow.

When she wrapped her arms around him and her naked thigh brushed his bare thighs she realized he'd been very busy and she smiled. "You work quickly."

"I beg your pardon, but I gave you two months to remove my clothes and you kept saying 'Wait until we get married,' and so now we're married and—"

She scooched up and kissed him, if only to shut him up, but he enveloped her in his strong arms and her breasts cushioned themselves in the thick mat of hair on his chest. She sighed with pleasure and closed her eyes.

The flicker of the lamp danced behind her eyelids as his hands roamed over her body and her hands played on his shoulders, slid down his arms, then roamed and explored anywhere and any way they wanted. Their legs braided as their hands caressed and they kissed a long, warm kiss that didn't seem to have a beginning and didn't need an end. There were no doubts. There were no questions. There was only one man and one woman and one answer tonight. And when he rolled her to her back and looked into her eyes with the expression of love she wanted only from him, her eyes pooled with tears again.

"I'm going to love you forever, you know," she whispered.

"That's exactly what I've been waiting to hear."

*   *   *   *   *

SILHOUETTE
Desire™

COMING NEXT MONTH

#571 SLOW BURN—Mary Lynn Baxter
Lance O'Brien's kidnapping was over in a moment. Marnie Lee was
left to deal with the aftershock—and with Lance's father, Tate
O'Brien, a most enticing captor himself.

#572 LOOK BEYOND THE DREAM—Noelle Berry McCue
Erin Kennedy was surprised to land a job at a California health
club—and when she met her blue-blooded boss, Logan Sinclair, she
knew her wildest dreams had come true.

#573 TEMPORARY HONEYMOON—Katherine Granger
Overefficient Martha Simmons was just doing her job when she
agreed to temporarily marry her boss, Jake Molloy. But once they
said their "I dos," she hoped permanent love would follow.

#574 HOT ON HER TRAIL—Jean Barrett
Beth Holland was hiking the Appalachian Trail to save precious land
from destruction. Opposition came in the form of sexy Brian
McArdle.... Could he sidetrack Beth *and* walk away with her heart?

#575 SMILES—Cathie Linz
Classy dentist Laura Peters was haunted by fears of failure—until she
met roguish Sam Mitchell, who taught her to believe in herself and to
smile her doubts away.

#576 SHOWDOWN—Nancy Martin
Manhattan attorney Amelia Daniels came to Montana to find her
runaway daughter and ended up in the arms of June's *Man of the
Month*, charming, irascible cowboy Ross Fletcher!

AVAILABLE NOW:

#565 TIME ENOUGH FOR LOVE
Carole Buck

#566 BABE IN THE WOODS
Jackie Merritt

#567 TAKE THE RISK
Susan Meier

#568 MIXED MESSAGES
Linda Lael Miller

**#569 WRONG ADDRESS,
RIGHT PLACE**
Lass Small

#570 KISS ME KATE
Helen Myers

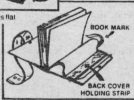

®️ *Silhouette Romance*®️

Homeward Bound

A duo by Laurie Paige

There's no place like home—and Laurie Paige's delightful duo captures that heartwarming feeling in two special stories set in Arizona ranchland. Share the poignant homecomings of two lovely heroines—half sisters Lainie and Tess—as they travel on the road to romance with their rugged, handsome heroes.

A SEASON FOR HOMECOMING—Lainie and Dev's story...coming in June.

HOME FIRES BURNING BRIGHT—Tess and Carson's story...coming in July.

Come home to A SEASON FOR HOMECOMING and HOME FIRES BURNING BRIGHT...only from Silhouette Romance!